Cheryl Sher...
May 196...

Candle
in the wind

(Original Title: ANNUZZA)

by HERTHA SEUBERLICH

Cover by Moneta Barnett

SCHOLASTIC **SBS** BOOK SERVICES

Published by Scholastic Book Services, a division
of Scholastic Magazines, Inc., New York, N. Y.

CONTENTS

*"Light a candle in the wind;
if the wind blows it out,
nevertheless you lit it."*

Romanian Folk Saying

Chapter 1

ANNUZZA BEGINS HER STORY

M Y HOME is in a Romanian village at the foot of the Carpathian Mountains. The wind blows down from the green beech woods, skimming the golden sea of corn and the maize fields, and it smooths the meadows into silk. The mountains lie westward and once the wind has reached the village, there is nothing to stop it from sweeping across the great plains of Bucovina and Moldavia which stretch to the east. The nearest big town, which stands on the Prut River, is nearly half a day's journey away. Our own river is the Siretul.

When I talk about my home, I mean first our distempered, pale yellow farmhouse, and our maize field. It is the biggest and the loveliest field in the village. In late summer, the stems wave high above my head and I can sit there for hours without being found. It is where I am writing now, hemmed in by the thick cornstalks, and the earth beneath me is warm and brown. I love to put my hand flat on the ground and pass it gently over the hard ridges. This earth is ours, Father's and Mother's, Puiu's and mine. Kuza had a share in it too until she got married, but now she has her own home.

The maize gives me cover just as the dense beech woods nearby close round the creatures who make it their home, and I feel safe here. But I ought not to be here at all. I should be in the big kitchen at home, giving the *mamaliga* a stir. *Mamaliga* is a thick broth made from maize flour and water, the staple food of us Romanian peasants. But once I am in the house, I am not allowed to read or write. Father and Mother are furious if they see me with a book or pencil and paper. They want me to come back to the village for good and marry Marcel — when I'm older, of course — and be a good peasant's wife. But I have other dreams, dreams as gay as the colored Easter eggs that stand all the year round on a wooden dish on the window sill. My dreams are as weird as the Persian carpet in Father Stanescu's parlor, and they can be dangerous too, for they have the power to bewitch me, to turn me suddenly into something I am not.

That is why I have decided to write the story

of my life, to try to describe the person I used to be and the one I am today.

I have spent a long time wondering where to begin, but now I know. I am leaning against a hard pumpkin. All around me, the corn is ripe and the sky is blue. The corncobs are yellow, with every grain a tiny nugget of gold. I loosen a handful of grains from one of the cobs and crunch them slowly between my teeth. They taste of milk and sugar and harvest.

It is five years since I first hid myself here among the maize, daydreaming. I was eleven years old then and I can remember it all so clearly. I was lying there in the ripe corn, just as I am now, and I dreamed that I was beautiful, as beautiful as Kuza, my elder sister. It sounds like a modest little dream compared with the dreams I have now, but it led to the transformation of my life and that is why I shall begin there.

I am writing it for Nadine and Nelo, and for myself too, a little.

Now that I am sixteen and look back, it seems to me that my life really began that day, with its modest little dream and the dreadful injustice I was made to suffer.

My name is Annuzza Burda, and I am the daughter of a peasant. Our farm is the biggest in the village and I am very proud of it. Everyone shares in the work on a farm, and even as children, the jobs we were given were as important in their way as rain and sunshine in season are for the crops.

On my eleventh birthday, Mother gave me the poultry to look after. I had to clean out the hen house, feed the hens, collect the eggs, and see that the little coop and the wired-off hen-run were properly locked. It was a responsible charge, for we had forty hens, lots of yellow chicks, and three aggressive cocks. Mother sold the eggs when she went to market in the town.

The poultry yard was closed in at the top with fine wire netting to protect it from the hungry birds of prey that were always hovering round the village. Only a few days before, I had noticed a greedy buzzard over the farm itself. It circled and looped through the air with wings outspread. Father had nailed a dead hawk to a long pole above the hen house in the hope that it would frighten the other birds, but it did not seem to have much effect on them. So before I went to school each morning, I had to make sure that the small wooden door into the hen-run was securely bolted. If the hens got out into the garden, there was no wire netting to protect them.

Things went smoothly for several months, until one day there was an accident. I got up as usual at six o'clock that morning. I did not need an alarm clock, for when I heard the farm wagon rumbling through the yard, I knew that Father

and Mother and my sister Kuza were setting
out for the fields and it was time for me to get up.

I jumped out of my wooden bed feeling happy,
and put on my white linen blouse and my skirt.
Our peasant skirts are called *katrinza,* and Mother
and Kuza had several with gay embroidery or
woven patterns, but mine was quite plain and not
at all pretty. Mother had promised me an embroidered one before long. When I was grown
up like Kuza, I intended to have a different one
for every day of the week as she did.

As soon as I was ready, I took a deep wooden
dish from the kitchen and filled it with hen food.
Then I went round to the back of the house,
where the slate roof comes down almost to the
ground and there is room to stack wood for the
winter beneath it. Not far away was the well. A
few quick turns of the wooden wheel at the side
were all that was needed to bring a brimming
bucketful of clear cold water to the top.

I put the wooden dish down on the ground
and bent over the edge of the well cautiously.
Father had roofed it over. The first narrow sun-
beam of the day fell across the yard to where I
stood. I could hardly see the water, it lay so deep.
"Annuzza!" I called down the well. My name
echoed dully from the depths of the shaft. Then I
remembered that I ought to be feeding the hens.

Near the well stood a paunchy rain-butt. We
always used rain water for washing ourselves and

our clothes. The water in the butt was as smooth as the mirror that hung on the wall near Kuza's bed. I leaned over and looked at myself. Did I really look like that, I wondered. I saw black hair parted in the middle, braided and wound round my head, but my braids were not nearly as thick as Kuza's. My eyes were dark brown and looked rather sleepy. They ought to be as blue as the morning sky overhead, I thought; then I'd look prettier. And my nose was much too big. My skin was the pinkish-brown of newly cut timber. It should have been as white as new milk. No, I should never be as lovely as Kuza.

I picked up a stone and flung it into the water, so that the eddying circles shattered the portrait I disliked so much, the picture of myself. I washed myself so hurriedly that my hands and face were still damp as I bent down to retrieve the hen food. I ran barefoot across the yard and pushed open the door. The hens flocked around me.

"Don't push so!" I called out sternly. "Go back, Mikuza! You don't have to be first every time. Leave something for the others!"

Mikuza was our best laying hen. She was snow-white and very valuable. You would really think that she knew it too, for she bossed the others mercilessly, even the cocks.

I let the corn trickle through my fingers, a shower of tawny rain. When I had shared out all the food, I went to look for the eggs. There were forty of them, big and warm. Mother would be pleased, I knew. Next, I filled the little troughs with fresh water and swept up the dirt with a broom. Meanwhile the sun had risen higher and it was time for me to be on my way to school.

I closed the wooden door behind me and put the padlock in position. Then I shook the little door hard, as I always did, to make sure that it was firmly closed and that nothing could happen.

It was a particularly lovely autumn day, I thought to myself. The air smelled pure and clean. Soon the church bells would start ringing. I got my schoolbooks, put them in the linen satchel I used, which I had woven myself, and I hurried off. I hummed softly as I left the farm. Every single day I used to feel glad about school. I was good at my lessons and the teacher said that I could be top of the class if I tried.

The song I hummed was one I had made up myself. It wasn't much, perhaps, but I thought it was rather nice.

> *Tomorrow is our harvest time*
> *In the sunny weather.*
> *Tomorrow is our harvest time*
> *The corn cobs fall together.*
>
> *When evening comes the moon will shine*
> *On all the peasants dancing.*
> *We shall dance till night is done*
> *And gray of dawn's advancing.*

Yes, tomorrow we'd be cutting the maize and in the evening there would be the *klaka*. The *klaka* is a great event, for it means not only a gathering of neighbors to help each other in a common task, such as bringing in the corn, but is a real festival, when people dance the whole night through. I thought it was the happiest celebration of the whole year. For the first time in my life, I was to be allowed to join in.

The church clock struck noon as I left the school with the other children. I ran on ahead, for I had something special to do. I wanted to get to the maize field. Once the corn had been cut, it would look bare and sad, and that was why it was important for me to go there for the last time that year.

I looked round for Puiu and saw him leaning against the whitewashed wall of a house a little way behind me. He was standing quite still, staring at a gypsy, who was sitting by the edge of the road, playing sad songs on his fiddle.

Puiu is my younger brother and he was eight then. He had a round face like Father's and his hair was cropped so short that it looked like the black down the sheep grow after the winter shearing. His eyes were dark and sometimes they looked cunning, sometimes defiant. Often he would sit down on a big stone somewhere and just gaze into space. When I asked him what he was doing, he would reply, "Nothing. When I'm

older I'm going to be a gypsy or a shepherd up
in the mountains. They can sit still all day and
do nothing at all."

I was glad that Puiu had not noticed me. He
might have wanted to come with me, and I preferred to be alone.

School was far behind me, as I passed the
fields which began where the village ended. Our
maize field was farther still, but if I hurried, it
took only a few minutes. When I got there, my
cheeks were hot from running so fast. I lay down
on the dry earth. Nearby, a green and yellow
pumpkin bulged among its leaves which were
nearly as big as Father's black umbrella. Father
always planted pumpkins between the corn, for
he was a good farmer and knew how to make
the most of the soil.

I leaned my head on the pumpkin. If I stretched
out one hand, I could reach a corncob. I love
even the word maize. It is a homely word, and
it sounds right for us peasants and it fits the
countryside too.

The sky above my head was like a cloth of blue.
I closed my eyes and a picture of my sister Kuza
flashed inside my head.

I admired Kuza more than I did Mother or
Father. Kuza was as beautiful as the golden icon
of the Virgin Mary that hung in the kitchen above
the wooden settle. Privately, I thought Kuza might
even be a little prettier. Her hair glistened like

yellow corn. Her braids were as thick as your
arm and she pinned them round her head. Her
eyes were as brown as the earth and her skin
was as white as new milk, but I've said that before.

I dreamed away into the distant blue of the
sky, imagining that I was as beautiful as Kuza
and that tomorrow I should dance the *hora*, our
national dance, as lightly as she.

I really ought to have been going home. It
must have been dinner time and probably the
food had already been dished out and was standing waiting on the bare wooden table in the
kitchen. But I was hooked as fast in my dreams
as the little fishes are that swallow the bait when
Father goes fishing.

I loved dreaming among the corn. . . .

"Annuzza, Annuzza!"

Mother's voice suddenly rang out through the
warm noonday air. I held my breath and did not
move. There was no breeze to sway the thick
stalks and no one near to betray my hiding place.

"Aaa-nnuzzaaa!"

Mother called my name over and over again.
But it was not her usual voice. It seemed angry
and urgent. I thought it would be wiser not to
ignore it.

I got up cautiously and ran, doubled over,
through the stems of corn and the pumpkins until
I reached the path. Nobody in the village wore

shoes in the warm weather. The soles of my feet were as brown and tough as leather and I did not feel the little stones in the hard-baked earth.

The footpath led straight to the farm, and from it I could see the wooden veranda that ran round the house. Peasant farmhouses usually have a veranda running round, and ours was light and clean and about a yard wide. Father had built a new one that spring, for the old one was rotten with age. The boards reached to my shoulder then, but I am not very tall even now — only five foot, four — and I am sixteen. There was an opening in the fencing facing the kitchen door in the center of the house. At each corner and at regular intervals there were tree trunks, stripped of their bark, that supported the low roof.

Mother was standing on the veranda, motioning me to hurry. Her outline filled the dark doorway into the kitchen. It was not like her to gesticulate so violently. Something must have happened.

I ran as fast as I could. The gate at the entrance to the courtyard stood wide open. My feet sank into the deep ruts which the cart wheels had made and I felt as if I were running along a gutter. I would have to tell Mother that I had been in the meadows seeing to the cows.

But I had no time to say anything. Mother came toward me and her face was so hard that it reminded me of a door that has been firmly

locked. I had seen her look like that only once
before in my life. That was the previous summer
when Puiu had thrown a dead cat down the well
and Father had had to drain it completely. It
was back-breaking work and it took him several
days. Puiu got a good hiding from Father, and
Mother forbade him to go to see old Drago, the
village shepherd, for a whole year. Mother knew
very well what a severe punishment that was,
for there was nothing Puiu liked better than to
be with Drago and his sheep, listening to the
legends and stories that Drago told so well.

"Come with me," said Mother sternly.

Where? What is it? I wanted to ask, but there
was a strange lump in my throat. I could not ask
questions, I could not even speak. Mother strode
ahead of me round to the back yard. Her footsteps were swift and angry.

Although I knew that I hadn't done anything
wrong, I was frightened, more frightened even
than when Father had been drinking and the
blue veins stood out in his forehead. But I haven't
done anything, I kept telling myself anxiously.

When Mother reached the hen-run, she stopped.
Turning toward me, she pointed silently to the
narrow door in the wire netting.

I could not understand what she was driving at.

"The door was open," she said at last.

Open? The door? But that wasn't possible!

"And the buzzard got Mikuza and two of the

chickens," Mother's voice went on. It was no louder than usual, but it sounded so harsh.

Mikuza, I thought. It had to be Mikuza, of course! And then it occurred to me that the door had no business to be open.

"Who left it open?" I asked.

"You," said Mother curtly.

"Oh, no!" I cried. "No, Mother. I didn't . . ."

"It can't have been anyone else," Mother interrupted me. Her eyes were as cold as ice.

"But I didn't do it. I know I didn't . . ." I stammered. Why did Mother look at me as if she despised me? Why didn't she let me explain first? That hurt most. I had always carried out my tasks most conscientiously. "But Mother," I protested again, "I put the padlock through when I . . ."

"That was yesterday or the day before." Mother did not let me finish. "Not today."

"The door was open," said Puiu.

I turned my head. Puiu was just behind me, grinning. He seemed to be relishing the fact that this time I was in trouble, not he. I could have hit him. I wanted to shake Mother and make her listen to me. I wanted to rattle the fence and make the hens speak up. Why couldn't they talk? They knew that I had put the padlock on as I did every day. But Mother wouldn't believe me. I started to tremble. All the gray clouds in the world floated before my eyes. I did not know what they would do to me.

"But it isn't my fault . . ." I whispered.

"Telling lies makes it worse," said Mother.

I wanted to shout at the top of my voice, "I'm not lying! I'm not lying!" But it wouldn't have been any use.

"Perhaps Puiu . . ."

"I was at school," he declared, and his grin grew wider. It was all very well for him to laugh. He was out of it.

"Or maybe Bunika fetched an egg . . ." I tried once more.

"Puiu! Bunika!" said Mother. "No. You did it."

There were tears in my eyes and my throat was choked. "Mother, I swear . . ."

"Be quiet!" Mother ordered harshly. "Go to the kitchen and wait for me there," and as she said it, she made a movement with her hand as if she were going to slap my face.

I ducked and bumped against the edge of the well. I held one arm in front of my face as I ran round the corner so that Mother and Puiu should not see my tears. It must have been Puiu or Bunika. I hadn't left the door open. The buzzard had killed Mikuza. Mikuza was dead. That was worse than the cat in the well.

Bunika, my grandmother, was sitting on the wooden settle in the kitchen. I panted hard as if I had been running fast. But it was only grief and anger and the false accusation that stuck in my throat.

"Bunika," I asked her hastily, "Bunika, have you been out to the hens today?"

"Not today and not yesterday. Poor Mikuza, the poor wee soul!" muttered Bunika. It seemed to me that her small eyes gleamed with cunning.

"But I hung the padlock up before I went to school," I cried.

"Then it must have been the Devil — or else it was the priest." Bunika's voice sounded malicious.

Tears streamed down my cheeks. I could not hide them any longer. No one believed me, no one. Mikuza was dead and I had to take the blame. I had no idea what would happen now and what Father would do to me when he came home. I never knew till then that such fear existed in the world. I stood there in the middle of the kitchen and all I could think was that I was being blamed for something I had not done and that I was terribly afraid.

Through the open kitchen door I could see Puiu in the yard. He had a handful of pebbles and he was chucking them against the slats of the fence. Every time he scored a hit, he crowed "Hurray." He could afford to play and laugh as if nothing had happened. I wanted to go out and push him.

Then Mother came indoors holding a bunch of feathers in her hand. Long white feathers they were, and little yellow ones too. She said nothing but held them out in front of me, all that was left of Mikuza and the chickens.

"Feathers," mumbled Bunika. "No more eggs — only feathers."

"Go to your room and get your satchel, Annuzza," said Mother, looking past me in the direction of the hearth.

I stepped toward her. "Mother, please believe me . . ."

"Go at once," said Mother.

"Mikuza's dead . . . dead, dead, dead," sang Puiu from the yard.

"But it isn't my fault!" I cried.

"A lie is as heavy as a cross to bear," said Mother in a caustic voice. "Do as I say."

I turned away slowly and went through the parlor into the small room I shared with Kuza. Over the chest in which I kept my clothes there hung a small icon. There was one in every room in the house. I knelt down and folded my hands. Was there no one to help, no one at all? My head rested on my fingertips. My hands were hot and wet and I could not stop crying.

"Dear God," I prayed, "I didn't do it. You know I didn't. Please make Mother believe me. . . . Please!"

The room was still, but outside Puiu was singing over and over again, "Mizuka's dead . . . dead, dead, dead," and the pebbles bounced against the fence in time to the chant. Mother must be waiting in the kitchen, deciding my punishment.

My linen satchel lay on the wooden chest. I

held its cool surface to my face for a moment and then went back to the kitchen.

"Here's some bread and bacon for you," said Mother. "It will last you three days."

What did she mean? There was the harvest tomorrow and the dance in the evening. . . .

"You'd better go up to the mountain pastures and stay with Drago for a bit. Come back in three days' time."

"But we're cutting the maize tomorrow, Mamika. You promised me I could go to the dance this year . . ." Normally I called her Mother, but now the familiar endearment, Mamika, came tumbling out.

"Pack the food and be off with you before Father comes home. I expect they'll get the maize cut and have the dance without your help. They've always managed so far."

It can't be true, I thought. I must have fallen asleep in the maize field. It is only a hideous nightmare. But the bag on my arm with the bread in it was real enough. It weighed as heavy as a millstone.

"The harvest dance is very noisy," said Mother grimly. "You'll find it quieter up in the hills, and you'll have more time to think things over in peace — how to fasten a hen-run, for instance. And you can press a cheese for us while you're there and bring it back when you come."

"Yes, it will be lively here at the *klaka*," came

Bunika's voice from the settle. "Up in the pastures, it will be very still."

"It gets dark quite early," said Mother. "You'd better be on your way. You've a fair distance to go."

So I was to be sent away by myself. That was no dream in the maize field. I left the kitchen with heavy steps. The veranda creaked like Bunika's voice. Outside Puiu was still croaking his song like a raven. The grass was gray from the long drought, and the soil pricked my naked feet. I must hurry, I thought; I must hurry.

Chapter 2

IN THE MOUNTAIN PASTURES

THE MOUNTAIN PASTURES were a little nearer heaven than our village. The path that led there was in a hurry to get away from the farms. It ran dead straight between wheat fields as far as the beech forest. Then it vanished among the tall tree trunks to reappear at the far edge of the woods where the green upland meadows began. It wasn't altogether easy for the path. It had to climb quite steeply, and it was much lonelier than the other paths around the village. Only rarely did a peasant or his wife climb the hillside to get a cheese made of ewes' milk, which Drago had pressed in his humble wooden hut.

All the way there I could think of nothing but Mikuza and the injustice of it all. By the time I got

back to the village the harvest celebrations would
long be over. The fat yellow corncobs, stripped of
their leaves, would be hanging to dry from the
edge of the roof over the veranda. And next day,
when everyone would be dancing the *hora* or listening to the ballads and laments we call *doina,*
I should not be able to hear the violin and the
voices. For me there would be only the rustling of
beech leaves and Drago's lonely shepherd flute.

I felt the tears running down my cheeks again.
If only Drago could tell me who had opened the
door of the hen-run! Drago knew so many things,
and others he seemed to guess instinctively.

It was somber and still in the forest. Not a beast
stirred. They must have been hiding in the under-
growth, waiting for me to pass so that the forest
would be theirs alone once more. I looked up.
The blue of the afternoon sky seemed to be embroidered with countless green beech leaves. The
treetops nodded toward each other and their
branches were entwined like the arms of young
men and girls dancing the *hora.*

> Come, my dear, and dance with me
> While the fiddle's playing.
> Dance and sing the whole night through
> To the music swaying . . .

Was I actually singing? I wiped my cheeks with
the back of my hand. What was the use of cry-

ing? The forest was as lofty as our church and
people don't cry in church, Mother once told me.

No, I must stop thinking about it and stop
feeling sorry for myself, too. I knew that I hadn't
done it, and perhaps one day Mother and Bunika
would know it too.

The forest ahead of me grew light. The beech
trees framed the pasture land as if it were a huge
green wreath crowning a head of fair hair. There
were so many sheep feeding on the grass that
their backs rippled softly as a sea of wool.

I looked for Drago but it was only when I was
halfway to his weathered little hut that I saw him
sitting on the bench outside it. He was leaning
on his sturdy shepherd's crook.

"Good evening, Drago!" I called out to him at
the top of my voice.

He lifted his head thoughtfully and looked
toward me. I could not tell whether he was glad
that someone had come to see him in his solitude,
or if I was intruding.

"Hello, Annuzza," he replied as I approached
the hut. "Is it the wind that has blown you here?"

"No, it wasn't the wind," I answered; "it was the
buzzard."

"Which one?" asked Drago. He stood up, tall
and lean, before me. The sheepskin cape that
peasants wear hung from his shoulders, and he
wore a tall, pointed hat of white lambskin. His
face was furrowed and his eyes were a bluish-

green and very lively. I was great friends with
Drago now, but when I was a little girl I used
to be afraid of him, for his nose was long and
hooked like the sharp beak of a bird of prey. I
had always been scared of them, and now one of
them had been responsible for killing Mikuza and
for causing me so much grief.

As I told Drago all that had happened, I could
feel my eyes brimming involuntarily.

"Tears don't usually mean much," said Drago,
"just that we're feeling sorry for ourselves." He
looked at me slyly. "You did forget to bolt the
door, didn't you?"

"No, really, Drago. I know I closed it. But
Mother won't believe me."

"Oh, it must have been you," insisted Drago.
"Probably you just forgot."

"No, no!" I cried. "Someone else must have
opened it after I'd gone. But I don't know who
it was. Can't you tell me, Drago? You know so
many things."

"All I know is that the day is long and that
the night is longer. I know that sheep often have
more sense than people. But I don't know who
left the hen house open, indeed I don't. . . ."

"Please try to think, Drago," I begged, and I
laid both hands on his arm.

"But I simply don't know what happened,"
murmured Drago. "How can I find out the truth?"

"It must have been someone who knows our hen-run."

"Or a gypsy child," suggested Drago. "They can smell things out, even a fox in its earth."

"Of course!" I exclaimed in great excitement. "It must have been a gypsy child. I must run straight home and tell Mother. It must have been a gypsy!" I turned to run back to the village at once.

But Drago held me back. "You don't know for sure, do you? It's possible, but it isn't certain. Your mother will never believe you."

My hands dropped heavily. Drago was right. Mother would believe it as little as my other protestations. I could not prove it.

"But it's so unfair, Drago," I whispered in dismay.

"Injustice is something that goes with us through life, like the priest and his surplice or Moishe, the village shopkeeper and his *kaftan*. We all have to put up with injustice at some time or other, and we all commit it in our turn too. Life isn't fair, but you must learn to accept it."

I heard his words, but I did not understand them.

"Come here, Annuzza," said Drago. "Sit by my side."

Drago felt in his pocket and took out his flute. People in the village said that Drago had made it himself and its pitch was certainly unusual. He put the instrument to his lips and started playing. It was not a song nor even a tune, but I thought that the sheep raised their heads to listen. It sounded like the wind in the trees, the birds singing, and the chime of countless little bells. But it was only Drago's flute.

Soon the sun set and the shadows of the trees melted silently into the darkness of the evening.

Drago put his flute away. "It's supper time, Annuzza," he said and he took me inside his hut. There was a jug of ewes' milk on the bare table and as I took the bread and bacon from my satchel, Drago lit the kerosene lamp that swung to and fro from a hook over the open hearth. The room it lit up was small and simple. The walls were made of bare logs, not even plastered. Against one wall stood two bunks with sacks of yellow straw for mattresses. There was a cracked wooden bench drawn up to the table. Above the hearth a round copper cauldron was suspended from a black iron chain and it gleamed smooth and golden-red where the light from the lamp caught it. In one corner hung a small icon.

It was a room in which I always felt at home immediately.

Drago sat down opposite me, but I did not speak to him. My thoughts were tugging me home. It would be supper time there too. Father might just be telling one of his stories about his military service and Puiu would be ready to prompt him with yet another question so that he did not stop. Mother and Kuza and Bunika and the two farmhands would listen in silence as they always did, but I would not be there. I had been sent away in disgrace. The bread tasted dry, not at all like the bread at home. I was not hungry in spite of my long walk.

"Do eat and drink, Annuzza," said Drago, and his voice was warm. I looked at him. He was leaning across to me, his arms flat on the table, one on each side of the plate piled with bread. How long and white his hair was! It reached almost to his shoulders. I don't know what it was about him, but I felt that I could go on looking at him forever.

"I'll tell you a story," he said suddenly. "Perhaps it will help you to understand what I meant about injustice."

How did Drago know that I had not understood him before? Could he guess everything that was going on in my mind?

"When I was about as old as you are now," he said, "there was no school in our village. We children used to work in the fields and indoors as farmhands and servants. When autumn came I used to play one of my favorite tricks. We had no pumpkins of our own so I stole one or two from the neighbors. I hollowed them out and cut faces in them — the faces of the farmers who swore at

me and punished me because I did not work fast
enough for them. Then I would spike the pumpkins on the rails of a fence for all the village to
see. Sometimes the faces were like enough for
people to tell whom they were meant to be. I was
never caught, but everyone knew that it was I
who stole the pumpkins and stuck them up by
the roadside.

"One day, a valuable icon disappeared from
the house of a farmer who had treated me particularly harshly. He was furious and sent for me,
declaring that I had stolen the icon. I had done
no such thing, but I did not know how to prove
it. The villagers all banded together against me
and called me a thief. They said that they knew
I kept stealing their pumpkins, and they marched
in a body to my parents' hut at the edge of the
village and insisted on searching it.

"They did not find anything, for there was nothing to find. But I had been given a bad name and
no one would give me work after that. Day after
day I tried to find the thief on my own and at
night I lay on the wooden bed near the fireplace
in the kitchen and I wept. Wherever I went, people
called me 'The Thief.'

"I couldn't stand it long. Even my parents did
not believe in me and would not speak to me any
more. So one day, I tied a few things into a bundle
and set out for the town. In the town, so I thought,
no one would know me and no one would call me

a thief. I would make a career for myself and one day I should return to the village, holding my head high. . . ."

Drago paused. He sat there for a few moments without speaking. His eyes did not see me, nor even the room where we sat. The oil lamp barely moved, the room lay half in darkness.

I sat there with my legs drawn up on the hard seat. I was as moved as if Drago's story were my own. I thought I could see the boy Drago before me, bewildered and forsaken. He looked rather like Puiu, I imagined, and his mother's face was as hard as Mamika's today when she sent me up into the hills. The town! Perhaps I should make for the town too. . . .

"Go on, Drago. What happened in the town?"

"In the town?" repeated Drago softly, as if he were talking to himself. "Everything was so big and strange in the town. No one called me a thief, but no one called me Drago either. No one gave me a piece of bread and the pavements were too hard to sleep on. Whenever I looked for work, people asked me what I could do. All I knew about was weeding and hoeing, tending the cattle, cutting the grass or the corn. That was no use in the town. People there talk so much too, much more than we peasants do in the country, and it was often difficult to grasp what they meant. I was hungry and I was cold.

"Sometimes I carried trunks for travelers from

the railroad station to the cabs, and in the end I polished shoes in the street. When I was eighteen, I had to do my military service and they said that I was a good soldier. I even learned to read and write. When my time was over, I went back to my village. I had never forgotten the injustice they had done me as a boy, but I had forgiven them. I had learned how to accept things. My parents' wooden hut was even more dilapidated than it had been when I left. Father was dead and Mother was half blind, but I shall never forget the way her face lit up when I returned. 'Drago,' she said and her voice was trembling, 'Drago, why have you been away so long? They found the icon soon after you left. Gypsies had taken it. . . .'"

"What happened then? Did the farmers beg your pardon?"

"Pardon? They didn't know the word, Annuzza. No. They had simply forgotten me, practically all of them. No one remembered about the icon. I became a shepherd. I had my flock and I had my flute and a book of Goga's poems. I had a lot to think about and I had learned that if you haven't studied, you'll never make a success of life."

"But you're a good shepherd, Drago," I said, moving a little closer to him.

"I could have become a shepherd without wasting ten years in the city. If you want to go there,

Annuzza, you must be able not only to read and write, but to study, to study hard."

"But I don't want to go away. . . ."

"Oh, nearly everyone wants to go to the city. You'll want to by and by, you more than anyone."

I was not sure that I would want to go away, but suddenly I knew what I did want. To study, to read and write, and to learn how to accept injustice.

"We mustn't waste oil, Annuzza. Go to bed now," said Drago, rising wearily to his feet to put out the lamp. "Let the day have its end."

Yes, I thought, this day must have its end.

Those three days up in the mountains passed more quickly than I had thought possible. After his long talk on that first evening, Drago said hardly one word more to me than was strictly necessary. Occasionally he would play his flute or browse through the book of poems by Octavian Goga that he kept under his straw mattress. It was his only book.

From time to time he would read one of the poems aloud, as if to himself, and these verses fascinated me. I lay in the grass at his feet and let the sun play through my splayed fingers on to my face as I listened to him. My thoughts no longer wandered down to the village, to the harvest and the dancing. They stayed with me there in the meadow with Drago, the sheep, and the poetry.

"Do you know where Goga came from?" I asked Drago on the second day.

"He came from a poor village in Transylvania. He was a peasant's child like us, but he studied hard and became a great man."

He was one of us, a peasant too. He studied hard and he became a great man. I kept repeating Drago's words to myself.

I decided that I would learn the poems by heart until I knew them as well as Drago himself. So I asked him for the book and he handed it to me as if it were a precious jewel. The pages were crumpled and gray from much handling, but it was the first book of poetry I had ever touched in my life. Until then I had known only schoolbooks. I read verse after verse. I did not always understand what I read, but the words had the same ring as Drago's flute.

I had once been to a circus where there was a magician. With one wave of his thin wand he had turned a mouse into a dove. Goga was a magician like that for me. His poems told me of life in the city, and as I read I seemed to be standing in a street with tall stone houses all around me. Goga had suddenly turned me, Annuzza Burda, into a city child. My cheeks glowed and I forgot to milk the sheep. Time flew by.

"The day has plenty of hours for dreaming, An-

nuzza, but there is a time for work, too." Drago
stood in front of me, tall and straight as a tree.

"Yes, Drago," I said and ran into the hut to get
a pail. Even as I milked the ewes I kept thinking
about the poetry, trying to say it aloud. I wanted
to remember every single verse in that well-
thumbed book.

On the third and last day I had no time for
dreaming. I helped Drago to press a cheese between two heavy boards and he molded it in a
wooden ring so that it came out as round as a
wheel. I did the milking and took the pails to
the hut. At noon, I cooked *mamaliga* in the swinging copper cauldron and I cut the bread for the
evening meal.

So the sun had set and risen again three times
before I packed my bundle again. Drago wrapped
the cheese in a damp cloth and he placed it carefully on a little pad on my head. Then he came
outside with me. "Chin up, Annuzza!" he said.
"The buzzard will kill many a hen before you're
as old as I am!"

He stood there upright and tall as ever and
watched me go. I went along the same path that
had brought me to him three days before, but
now it seemed different. Or was it I who had
changed? I was no longer alone as I had been on
my way there. By my side went Drago the boy
as well as Drago the wise old shepherd, but close
by my other side walked Goga the poet. So I had

two companions and my heart was light. What
was more, I had an aim in life. I was going to
study, and one day I too might leave for the
city. But it would not be in secret and ignorance
as Drago did it those many years ago. It would be
to do as Goga did — to make a name for myself.

> *Beyond the yellow fields*
> *And the lush woods,*
> *There, where the near horizon*
> *Blurs into shadow,*
> *Frowning and somber*
> *There lies the town.*
>
> *Between its stone walls*
> *Which lie in wait for us strangers*
> *Crowds bustle and throng,*
> *The poor and the rich*
> *The stupid, the clever,*
> *And some will go hungry*
> *To bed tonight.*

The round cheese swayed with every step and
I had to steady it with one hand, for I had my
empty linen satchel in the other one. I did not
think about the path. I thought only of the sounds
and the words of the poem that I kept saying
softly to myself, over and over again. *Beyond
the yellow fields* ...
So I mused, and I did not know then that one

day I should actually feel grateful to the buzzard, because otherwise I might never have gone to stay with Drago and the sheep, and the poet Goga.

Then the houses came into sight, small and squat as painted molehills, clustered together by the roadside. The church towered high above them as if it wanted to see over their heads. Smoke curled from a chimney here and there and was lost against the blue of the sky.

Was Mother still angry with me? And Father? I slowed down my steps. Now everything came closing in again—Mikuza, the buzzard, and my punishment, which had turned out to be no punishment at all.

If you carry a basket or a cheese on your head, you have to balance on your toes and keep your neck quite stiff. I was nearly home but my bare feet ached and my arm had gone to sleep. There was only a short stretch of wild fruit trees separating me from the farm, when crack! something hard struck against the cheese and I nearly dropped it. I wondered what it was and stopped to take the cheese off my head.

Mischievous laughter rang out from the thick leaves of the apple tree. I might have guessed. It was Puiu. Before I could scold him, he called, "Back again, Annuzza? They're all waiting for the cheese."

"If you're in such a hurry for it, you can carry it back to the house."

"Yes, I'd better," replied Puiu, jumping down to the ground. "When you see Father's face, you might drop it."

"What do you mean?" I asked.

But Puiu did not answer. He scampered off like a hare, carrying the cheese in both hands.

"Here she is!" I heard him yell as I came round the corner to the farm.

Father was in the kitchen, sitting at the bench behind the table, broad and massive as a log of wood. Clouds of thick smoke came from his long pipe so that I could hardly make out his face. Mother stood near the hearth laboriously stirring something in a pot.

"Yes, indeed. It is Annuzza," came Bunika's voice from the corner. I could not see her at all for the dense smoke from Father's pipe.

"Well? Have you brought Mikuza back?" asked Father in a loud voice.

"Leave her alone," said Mother.

"She's brought a cheese back," said Kuza, and it was only then that I noticed her. She was leaning against the parlor door and she looked at me kindly.

"Cheese! Cheese! What good is cheese when we need Mikuza?" shouted Father, getting to his feet. "You'll have to work, I tell you. I'll make you work so hard all winter that it will pay for another Mikuza in the spring. Do you hear what I say?"

When Father shouted, his voice carried right

through the farm and the horses in the stables pricked their ears. I bowed my head and felt quite small.

"Yes, Father," I said, "I'll work hard . . ."

"That's enough, Burda," called Mother from the hearth. "Shouting won't bring Mikuza back to life and Annuzza will do as she's told without all that noise."

"She'll work, she'll work," Bunika muttered, "and the winter is long."

I was longing to tell them what Drago had suggested, that it might have been a gypsy child who opened the door, but I held my tongue. Life isn't fair, but you must learn to accept it — the words still rang in my ears. Bunika was right. Winter was long with us, but not only for working hard. There would be time for studying and for dreaming too.

Chapter 3

THE STRANGER IN THE SLEIGH

F OR PEOPLE IN THE COUNTRY, the winter is like a sheltering roof. The family that would otherwise be out of doors all day in the fields is gathered together into one room, and although their industrious hands never lie idle, they do peaceful domestic tasks.

Every afternoon, Mother lit the oil lamp that hung down from the center of the ceiling and cast a circle of light round us all, enclosing us like one happy family. That is the way it had been every winter, but for the first time in my life, I started wondering if we really were a happy family.

It was rare for any of us to speak, and the kitchen was as silent as the fields outside, where the snow protected next year's harvest with a thick white blanket. In spite of the fire, the room felt cold because we did not talk to each other. I had never felt like this before, but after spending those days with Drago up in the hills, I knew how words can hearten and warm and help another person along. I realized that each of us was quite alone, full of his or her own private thoughts and inner life, even as we sat so close together on those winter afternoons. It was as if we were all out of touch and had lost the power of communicating with the others.

I often stole a glance at Mother who usually sat between Kuza and me, spinning. She held the hemp or the flax firmly in one hand and turned the wheel with the other. From the mass of single fibers emerged the linen thread that would be woven into clothes for us to wear. I watched Kuza too. She was knotting tufts of wool to make a carpet. It was intended for the parlor of her own home when she got married. The wool came from the sheep Drago looked after for us in the mountains, and Father had dyed it with home-made dyes from wild plants.

I spent the afternoons embroidering, but I was not working on the long-desired *katrinza* or a blouse for feast days. Beside me stood a little workbasket full of colored threads. I held a square of linen in one hand and a fine needle in the other, and I stitched away at a bright complicated

pattern which stood out against the whiteness of
the surface. It was a tablecloth, my second that
winter, and there were still two more to do.
Mother would take them all into the city in the
spring and sell them as Easter cloths. Father
hoped that the money they would bring would
pay for another laying hen.

In the corner by the window Father and Puiu
sometimes carved, and sometimes made pots. We
were all busy on those afternoons, all except
Bunika, who just sat there in her place below the
icon, with her shoulders hunched and her eyes
screwed up, glancing keenly from one of us to the
other. Now and again she told Puiu, "Put some
more wood on. It's getting cold."

If I were alone in the kitchen for a while, I
would sometimes look up from my work toward
the shelf near the window. There stood a blue
glass ball, which Father had brought back when
he had finished his military service. Inside the
thick glass you could see several tiny houses, a
church, and a street where a sleigh stood waiting
with its horses ready. Occasionally I lifted the ball
down and shook it and it began to snow inside
the glass. Small silvery flakes fluttered over the
roofs, sprinkling sleigh and horses.

The little glass ball had always seemed like
magic to me, and this winter I acquired a special
affection for it. I wove my dreams round it, as
Mother wove the thread she had spun into a piece

of linen. It must be just like that when it snows in the city, I fancied. I could see myself stepping into a waiting sleigh and driving through the streets, and I heard the tinkle of the little bells fixed to the harness. I longed to see it in reality one day — winter in the city with snow on the pointed roofs and the broad pavements. It seemed so lovely in my imagination.

What with embroidering and dreaming, there was not much time for studying during those first weeks of winter. Some evenings I read in secret when the moon shone bright as a lantern through the bedroom window. Kuza had gone to sleep long before and I could hear Father's loud snoring coming from my parents' bedroom. But it was then that I studied and read. Or I might lie awake with my eyes open, softly reciting Goga's poems to myself.

It was one day just before Christmas that something happened quite unexpectedly which gave a new point to my studying. It began by Mother deciding that I need not do my sewing that afternoon. She said that I could go back to school with the other children to practice carols, and it was there that something occurred which at first served only to feed my dreams, but later guided my life in a completely new direction.

As soon as dinner was over I folded up my sewing and put it away in the workbasket. My *opanken* were standing near the hearth. *Opanken* are like shapeless leather moccasins and we wear them out of doors in winter. They are clumsy but warm, and they keep your feet dry. My sheepskin cape hung on the hook near the veranda.

I wore thick black woolen stockings and it felt lovely to slide your feet into the *opanken* when they had been warmed near the fire. As I reached for my cape, Bunika looked up inquisitively.

"And where might you be going?" she asked.

"She's going to a carol practice at the school," answered Mother.

"The threads will lie idle in the basket and the tablecloth will stay white while she sings," remarked Bunika.

"If the children don't sing carols, joy will never cross the threshold and there will be no Christmas star," Mother replied.

"Good-bye!" I called. Then I slipped out, closing the door behind me and away I went into the crisp winter air.

The snow had been shoveled high on both sides of the path, which was trodden hard. I ran all the way to the village, and soon I could see the clock, shining like a gay sunflower in the church tower. I had plenty of time. I should have the school all to myself and I looked forward to it. Since I had made up my mind to study, school had become a second home to me.

The school building was low and white, and

from the outside it looked like any other village house, with two steps to the front door. On one of them sat Babull, as we all called him. He was a poor old man. His gray hair was long and always tousled as if he had just been out in a high wind. He had no home of his own and no possessions of any kind except the clothes he wore. He used to sleep on a rug in the school corridor and he kept the classrooms clean.

"Hello there, Annuzza! Where are you going?" he greeted me as I tried to get past him into the school.

"We're having a carol practice," I answered.

"There's plenty of time," said Babull. "The clock finger has to go a whole round before it starts."

"That doesn't matter," I said. "I can read while I'm waiting for the others to come. The time will soon pass."

"My goodness, you're talking like Mr. Morianu himself," said Babull, and shook his head in astonishment.

Mr. Morianu was the teacher. He came from the city and he wore a gray suit like the ones city people wore, a yellow shirt, and even a tie. Father was always saying that Mr. Morianu ought to wear peasant clothes, and that a town suit did not fit in with a village school. Father was against everything that smacked of the city. But I liked things as they were, and I did not see why Mr. Morianu should be expected to dress in a homespun smock and trousers with a leather belt, when he wasn't a peasant at all and did not even come from our village. He was a real gentleman from the town and even his way of speaking was quite different from ours.

I opened the door. The long corridor was empty. I had never seen it like that before. The two class-rooms lay to the left and right, and at the end was a high door that seldom opened for us children. That was the teacher's room.

My classroom was the one on the right. A piece of paper on which was written "Carol Practice" swung from the door handle. The room was as empty and silent as the corridor and I walked in on tiptoe, stealthily. I did not sit down in my own desk in the front row, but went straight past it to the teacher's rostrum. I was surprised to see how different the classroom looked the other way round.

I knew that no one would come for some time, so I sat down on the teacher's chair and sat up tall. I surveyed "my" class. There was Annuzza Burda, who was quite a clever child, and could recite several poems by Goga. Then came Maria Petrescu, the carpenter's daughter, who gave her-self airs because she wore real boots, black ones. Next to her was Marcel, the Burgomaster's son. Marcel was the tallest in the class and he was always the leader in the boys' games. I had to admit that he made a good captain and was always fair, but he was rather conceited and liked to show off. Maybe it was because he was descended from the Hun princes, or so he claimed. It could be true, though, for his eyes slanted a little in his long face with its high forehead, and his hair was as red as a fox's fur.

So I played at being the teacher, shaking my head over Maria, who did not know a single poem by Goga, lecturing the children about life in the city as I imagined it, taking Marcel down a peg or two, and giving Annuzza her due when she gave me the right answer, which was often.

Then a door creaked, voices spoke, and my dream came to an abrupt end. There was a harmonium standing near the desk which the teacher had borrowed from the church for the afternoon practice. I struck one of the keys as I had seen Mr. Morianu do. One lost note wailed out, like the cry of a baby owl in the night. I jumped down from the platform and hurried to my own desk. My heart thumped as if I had nearly been caught doing something wrong. But it was only that I had been daydreaming a little.

The classroom filled until it hummed like a beehive. Maria's black boots squeaked over the floorboards. The children all hung their sheepskin capes on the metal catches of the three windows, so that you could not see the glass at all. It was like any other day at school now, and I was only one of twenty-five pupils. My dreams had fled as if the loud voices all around them had frightened them away.

Again the door opened. This time it was Mr. Morianu. He did not waste any time, but sat down at the harmonium and lifted the lid. I looked at his hands and saw how white they were, not calloused with heavy work on the land like Father's. His touch on the keys was gentle and he played the melody with his left hand, while the little baton in his right hand danced lively figures in the air. Then he lifted his head and gave us the signal to start. The lovely Christmas carols filled the room, telling of the redemption of mankind and of the birth of the Saviour. As I sang with the others, I kept thinking about Christmas Eve.

In a tiny loft under the roof was the Christmas star that I had made last year. It was nearly as big as the wheel by the side of the well at the farm. It was covered with shining silver paper pasted on to thin wooden rods. From each point of the star hung a little silver bell and in the middle there was a space cut out big enough for a burning candle. On Christmas Eve, Puiu and Marcel and all the rest of us would go through the village singing Christmas carols and the bells would tinkle like sleigh bells in the town. As we passed from house to house, we were no longer just children. We were the *Colindatore de Stea*, the Singers of the Star.

On Christmas Day after church, the girls stayed at home, but the boys went round the village by themselves. We called them the Herod Singers then, and Marcel was their leader. They stopped at every door to sing carols about the Creation and about the slaughter of the babes at Herod's command. People gave them a few coins or a slice of Christmas cake.

I wondered if there were Herod Singers and Singers of the Star in the town.

All at once there was a knock at the door. Everyone stopped singing. Reluctantly, Mr. Morianu called out, "Come in!"

Babull stood there in the doorway. His face looked frightened and his crooked legs in their tight homespun trousers were trembling at the knees. He looked so ridiculous that some of the children giggled.

"Be quiet," ordered Mr. Morianu. "What is it, Babull?"

Babull nodded his head toward the teacher's room. "There's . . . there's someone in there," he stammered, "a distinguished gentleman from the city. He came by sleigh and he wants to speak to you, sir."

Mr. Morianu put the baton down on his desk, told us to behave ourselves, and followed Babull out of the classroom.

He had hardly closed the door when Marcel got to his feet. In one hand he held a rough plectrum and in the other his *cobza,* which is rather like a mandolin. He mounted the teacher's rostrum and began to play. He gave us one folk tune after another and all at once he seemed to have grown much older than the rest of us, as if he did not belong to the class any more. Maria, sitting next to me, gazed at him spellbound. I thought that she looked terribly silly, although I had to admit that I liked his playing very much too. All the same, I wouldn't just sit there staring at him as Maria did.

Marcel broke off abruptly and looked toward the door. We all turned and saw the teacher standing there. He looked nearly as agitated as Babull had, and he simply did not notice that Marcel was standing at his desk.

"Annuzzal" he called, beckoning to me. "Come with me."

Without another word, he strode ahead of me back to his room and I found myself standing in front of the "distinguished gentleman," as Babull had called him. I did not think that he looked so different from our teacher, except that he was dressed all in black. His suit, his shoes, his hat which he held on his knees, everything was black, even his tie. He looked like a stiff old raven, I thought to myself. His hands were as white as Mr. Morianu's and his shoes shone like the hearth at home when Mother had just finished polishing it.

I hid my hands quickly behind my back. They were so red and cracked that I was suddenly ashamed of them. I would have hidden my feet too, with their black woolen stockings and the shabby *opanken,* but I did not know where to put them.

The stranger looked me up and down as if he were thinking of buying me. I felt as if I were being inspected in the market place. I went red with embarrassment and then very pale. What had I done?

Mr. Morianu sat down at the long table opposite the visitor. Neither of them spoke. I could feel the silence weighing me down like the cheese I had brought back to the village from the mountains.

The strange gentleman went on looking at me. I tugged at my skirt in case it was crooked.

"So this is Annuzza Burda," he said at last.

"Yes, this is Annuzza," Mr. Morianu confirmed.

"Do you like school, Annuzza?" the gentleman asked me. His voice was low and you could not imagine him shouting the way Father and the other men in the village did.

"Yes," I said. Then I said it again, just "Yes."

"She never misses a single day," added Mr. Morianu, nodding at me in an encouraging way.

"Do you know what you would like to be when you grow up?" the man went on.

"Someone . . . someone famous," I stuttered, and as I said it, I clapped my hand in front of my mouth. What a stupid thing to say!

The strange gentleman laughed gently. "We all want to be famous when we are young."

Mr. Morianu nodded in agreement. There was a trace of a smile on his face, and I had a suspicion that both these city gentlemen were laughing at me.

"I am glad you said that, Annuzza," said my teacher. "One should always aim high in life if one wants to achieve anything. Do you know what I mean?"

"Yes," I said, "I think I do."

"Has it occurred to you that you might leave this village one day?" the stranger went on.

I wondered what he was driving at but I answered promptly enough, "Oh yes, I have often dreamed about it. . . ."

"Dreams alone won't get you very far. All the same," and here he turned to Mr. Morianu, "I think you are right."

What was he right about, I thought.

"You can go back to your class, Annuzza," said the teacher.

I turned to go and was about to leave the room when it crossed my mind that I ought to say

something before leaving. I hurried back to the
table and bobbed a curtsy, as I did to the priest,
and then I blurted out without thinking, "I've . . .
I've read some poems by Goga too!" Then I was
outside the door again.

I stopped for a moment in the corridor and
leaned against the wall. I was terribly excited. The
men were speaking softly behind the closed door.
I tried to listen but could not make out what they
were saying. All I could hear was the respectful
note in Mr. Morianu's voice, as if he were bowing
low after every sentence.

The door opened unexpectedly and I had to
squeeze myself into the nearest corner against the
wall. The stranger and the teacher went to the
front door with Mr. Morianu a step behind. The
gleaming black shoes of the gentleman from the
city squeaked as if they disapproved of the narrow, ill-lit corridor. I could see only their silhou-
ettes. Mr. Morianu opened the front door and
made a deep bow. There was a sleigh outside and
the stranger got into it. The teacher went on
bowing all the time, just the way Babull did in
front of Mr. Morianu, bowing and scraping whenever he spoke to him.

I still did not know what the visitor wanted, nor
what it had to do with me.

As the sleigh drove off, I hurried back to the
classroom. Maria, Marcel, and the others clamored

round me. Their questions flowed into each other like the little streams of water that crisscross through the soil after heavy rain.

Before I could answer, Mr. Morianu had come back. "Let us get on with the singing," he said simply. That was all.

An hour later, we all took our sheepskins from the window catches and started to go home. It was already dark out of doors. Mr. Morianu screwed down the wicks of the kerosene lamps. Just as everyone was jostling and pushing through the doorway, Mr. Morianu called me back.

I stood before him, an animated question mark.

He laughed. "You were quite overwhelmed, weren't you, Annuzza?" Then he said, "I want you to write a composition, and the title is 'My Dreams.' Have it ready for the beginning of next term, when we come back after the Christmas holidays."

"Is it . . . is it a punishment task, sir?" I asked.

"No, no. On the contrary. But time will tell. . . . And go on working hard, Annuzza, harder than ever."

"Yes," I said.

Then I was allowed to go.

There was no one about when I reached the road. I could see the feeble lights of the lamps in the houses nearby, for we had no electricity, only oil lamps or candles. Here and there, the snow glistened like clear water in the moonlight. It was very cold. Even my soft *opanken* made a crunching noise as if I were running over gravel.

Suddenly I heard a voice behind me. "Annuzza!" I turned round and there was Marcel. He had slung his sheepskin over his shoulders in the way the young men did on feast days. It was quite becoming, I thought. Marcel seemed more grown up than ever.

"I'll go part of the way with you," he volunteered. "I'm going to Munteanu's to get some honey."

I nodded.

"What did they want you for?" he asked.

I shrugged my shoulders.

"But they must have told you," he insisted.

"Is that why you waited for me?" I asked.

"No — yes — no . . . not really, Annuzza."

I had never heard Marcel stumble for words before and I had to laugh. That vexed him. He looked away and trampled down the snow as if he were crushing something underfoot.

"I have to write an essay," I said quickly.

"How silly," was Marcel's reaction.

"It is, isn't it?" I agreed.

That was the whole of our conversation. I wanted to be alone just then and think things out. I felt as if a storm were brewing.

When we reached the farm, I said, "Good night, Marcel."

"Good night, Annuzza," he replied and shook

hands with me as grownups do. We had never done that before. Everything seemed odd today. Before I went indoors, I turned my head to watch him. He was running back to the village like a dark shadow between the piled-up snow.

That's not the way to Munteanu's, I thought suddenly. Marcel's going the wrong way. . . .

Chapter 4

MY ESSAY

WE HARDLY EVER mentioned school at home, and when we did, it was never a pleasant topic. Father considered that reading and writing were quite unnecessary. He had never learned how and he did not see why his children should either. It seemed much more important to him that we should work all day in the house or on the farm. He abused the state roundly, even in public in the village, because it compelled parents to send their children to school.

Mother seldom said anything when Father aired his views, but her opinion was not very different from his. Reading and writing seemed useless to a peasant. From Mother's point of view, the thing that mattered was the practical running of the

farm and foretelling the weather by the flight of
a bird or the formation of the clouds. Simple
arithmetic was often important, admittedly, but
somehow everyone picked up enough to manage
— after a box or two on the ear, if necessary. That
was the way Mother and Father thought.

Their attitude was driven home to me very
forcefully a few days after the conversation in the
teacher's room at school.

I was alone in the house one afternoon. The rest
of the family had gone to help our neighbor,
Munteanu. The hemp yield had been so abundant
last harvest that the Munteanus had not finished
spinning it yet, so they had arranged a *klaka*. But
I had to stay at home and finish my second tablecloth. Those were Father's orders.

The kitchen seemed enormous to me that evening. My gaze kept wandering to the wooden settle
in the corner by the window. I could not quite
believe that Bunika was not there as usual. I had
the strange feeling that she was still keeping an
eye on me, so that my fingers did not tire too
readily over the embroidery.

My eyes looked up from the linen cloth to the
window. It was snowing. The flakes clung to
the panes like tiny stars. The fire crackled in the
hearth, and I was alone, nearly as alone as in the
ripening maize field.

I got up and took the magic glass ball carefully
from its shelf. I shook it with both hands and held

it against the firelight. It looked as if twinkling sparks were falling on the roofs of the toy houses.

In summer, my only dreams had been about being as pretty as Kuza one day. But now my thoughts wandered away to the city.

Suppose I started writing my essay today? "My dreams," I murmured softly to myself. I wondered if it would be hard to put on paper the bright pictures that kept flashing through my head. I felt the urge to find out right away.

I went through the best parlor on tiptoe as I always did to save the carpet. Not every farmhouse had a parlor and I was proud of ours. The floor was covered with rugs that Mother had made herself. She had woven the curtains too, and Father had painted the big beechwood cupboard with the identical patterns that I was embroidering on the tablecloths. On the walls were several photographs in narrow black frames. They had been taken when Father was in the army.

I wondered if the people in the cities had finer parlors in their houses. A beam of light from the kitchen fell on the golden icon which hung above the sofa. The sofa was our most valuable piece of furniture, and we were not often allowed to sit on it. My parents had bought it many years before in the town. On big festivals like Christmas and Easter we even had our meals in the parlor and that was tremendously exciting.

A small door led from the parlor into the bedroom I shared with Kuza. It was a modest room but I was always fond of it. I took down the linen satchel containing my school things and went whistling back to the kitchen. I was alone and the evening was mine.

Oh, I knew I was doing wrong as I put my sewing to one side on the settle by the hearth. My exercise book lay on the table before me, the inkwell stood to one side, and my fingers gripped my pen. They were trembling a little with excitement. The white pages were fascinatingly blank.

How should I begin? The first words were the hardest. Last Sunday, Father Stanescu had preached a sermon and he had said, "Once you have made a start, the rest of your work follows of its own accord like a stream which has found its course." The expression appealed to me, although Father thought that work is work at any stage — beginning, middle, or end. Nothing follows of its own accord. It just has to be done. Privately I thought that Father had missed the point.

I decided that I would begin my essay by quoting the sermon. My pen flew over the white paper. My dreams in the maize field, up in the hills, and in the schoolroom grew together into a story, as they came to life. In an instant I was as pretty as Kuza and Marcel brought flowers to my window secretly because he liked me. And one day, the stranger came in his sleigh and we drove off into the city. I went into a big building and there I could study all I wanted. I went from class to class until I knew everything that can be taught in a school. I could even write poems, poems as beautiful as Goga's. I was famous and one day it was my own sleigh that took me back to the village. But not for good, just for the holidays. And every time I brought presents for the family — beads and silks and satins — and, if Father wanted them, I could buy him a hundred hens.

All at once I started. I could hear the creaking of the boards on the veranda. Before I could get to my feet and hide my writing things, the door flew open and there stood Father in the dark doorway, bringing winter into the kitchen with him. Snow clung to his *opanken* and they looked like white galoshes. He was breathing heavily and his face was red. He was drunk.

I sat turned to stone.

"What are you doing, Annuzza?" he asked. He did not shout, not yet. But his voice vibrated menacingly.

I did not dare to answer.

"Well? I'm waiting!" said Father as he stepped nearer to the table.

"I'm writing something for school," I stuttered, and hung my head.

"And what about the tablecloth? Your work? Mikuza?" He was shouting now. His voice resounded from the wooden walls and he banged his clenched fist on the table so that the ink spurted from the bottle and the pen rolled on to the floor.

"I'll show you how to write when there's work to do!" he roared. He seized my exercise book, ripped it down the middle, and threw both halves into the stove, leaving the doors wide open.

"Don't, Father! Don't!" I cried, and ran to the stove. But the flames had already seized hold and were hugging the sheets of paper with their little red arms. The edges curled, turned yellow, then brown, and finally the sheets crumpled to pieces. My essay! I laid my head on the unfinished table-cloth and wept. Father grasped my shoulder with his hand and made me sit up.

"School's the place for writing!" he shouted, and shook me. I could see the oil lamp swinging violently in the draught from the open door. I wanted to get out of the kitchen, anywhere, away. But Father was still holding me, clutching my arm.

"In this house you'll work, do you hear? You're a peasant's daughter, that's what you are, and you're going to stay one too. There'll be no reading and writing here. This isn't the priest's house. Here you'll use your hands to work, and if you don't obey, you'll get out. Like this . . ."

As he said it, he gave me a push through the doorway. I stumbled over the veranda, down the two steps, and fell headlong into the snow. It was chilly and wet and I could feel it through my blouse. But I did not want to get up. I hated the smell of liquor on Father's breath, and I did not want to listen to the anger in his voice and the coldness in it that was icier than the snow.

"Wipe the ink up and get on with your work," Father ordered me.

I lifted myself slowly. My stockings were wet and there was snow clinging to my skirt. Father stood waiting in kitchen until I had started sewing again. Then he turned and went out without another word.

I was alone again, but my writing book had gone and Father had thrown my dreams into the fire with it.

But they would come back, I knew they would. Tomorrow or the next day they would be back, and I was going to write that essay, come what may. I would do it secretly by moonlight in my bedroom, or at school, when and where I could. Mr. Morianu would help me if I told him the truth.

My fingers groped for another thread and my needle went in and out of the linen. I had to obey Father but I would never give up my writing and studying, never.

Chapter 5

THE BLESSING
OF THE WATERS

K UZA WAS NOT ONLY BEAUTIFUL. She was good
and kind to me too. I told her about the
composition I had to write and she promised to
help me. Not with writing it, of course; that I had
to do myself. But she gave me a candle, and a
piece of cardboard to put over the window in our
bedroom so that the light could not be seen from
the yard when I was writing secretly at night before I went to sleep.

The day I finished my essay was the one on
which Father Stanescu visited all the houses in the
village dressed in his ceremonial robes and accompanied by the boys' choir and the sexton. He
entered the courtyard carrying a crucifix and holy

water. Puiu, who was waiting at the window, called out, "They're coming, they're coming!"

My essay was five pages long and quite different from the one I had written in the kitchen that day when Father took me by surprise. It seemed to me to be a particularly favorable omen that the priest came to bless our house on the very day that I finished my writing. He walked solemnly through the veranda and he blessed all the rooms in the house, the stable, the barn, and the poultry-run too. As he did so, the choir sang the *Kyrie Eleison*. It was all very impressive and dignified. As Father Stanescu stood in front of me to sprinkle me with holy water, I made a wish. It was that Mr. Morianu would be pleased with what I had written, and I hoped that it would come true. I had concealed my exercise book under my linen smock, so that the priest would really bless it too.

The farmer Munteanu followed the priest, and with the smoke from a long candle he painted the sign of the cross on the parlor ceiling. Then it was Father's turn to do the same at the house of our neighbor to the left.

Next day was January sixth, the Feast of the Three Kings. It was an important feast day with us, commemorating Christ's baptism by John the Baptist. On this day the Blessing of the Waters took place and we called it the Jordan Ceremony.

The men who had been given the honor of carrying the banners and the cross led the long procession down to the Siretul and then came the priest with the long line of people following behind. Kuza and Puiu and I walked side by side. I had my writing book hidden under my cloak and I intended to give it to Mr. Morianu when no one was looking.

The road from the church curved out of the village toward the river. We were among the last, so we could see virtually the whole column unwinding before us. Everyone wore the same kind of a light gray sheepskin, and the men carried their pointed sheepskin caps in their hands. It looked as if a tired, straggling flock were following its shepherd along the road.

We halted by the bank of the river where a few days before the men had built a tall cross of ice. It was hard work putting it up, but the men undertook it year after year and we always went to watch them.

Great lumps of ice were hewn out of the village pond and carried down to the river on ox-drawn sledges. There the ice was cut into shape. The men had done it for so many years that they knew the best way to go about it. They lit a fire of brushwood and heated lengths of wire in the flames. When these were hot enough, they were used to cut the ice and to trim it into the right size and shape. They needed three square blocks for the upright portion of the cross and one long, thick piece to make the arms. The most difficult thing was to get it all into position. For that they had to have thick ropes and strong arms.

Two of the massive cubes made the body of the cross and the oblong piece was balanced across them, with the third block hoisted on top for the head. It took several hours to get it right, but when it was ready, the mighty cross stood there on the river bank, visible from a great distance.

As we approached it now, it stood there glittering in the soft winter sunlight as if it had always been there and would remain for all time. Iridescent rainbows shimmered wherever the sun's rays caught it.

We stood in a wide semicircle around the cross, near which had been placed several large barrels of water, ready for the priest to bless. A carpet of straw had been spread for him to stand on and here he read the Gospel and the choir sang the responses. This was always considered the climax of the ceremony.

Then the priest blessed the water in the barrels, and to end the service, we all sang a hymn: "When Thou, O Lord, wast baptized in the Jordan." I kept looking round for Mr. Morianu and eventually I caught sight of him in his black city overcoat at the farther end of the crowd.

As the hymn died away, Father Stanescu, the sexton, and the banner bearers, who included Marcel's father, the Burgomaster, got ready to go back to the village. As they left, a few small mortars were let off and the bangs mingled with cries of "Chiraleisa," which is *Kyrie Eleison.*

But the rest of the villagers thronged round the barrels to fill the empty bottles they had brought with them so they could take home some of the water that had been blessed. I was watching Father and I saw him bend down to pick up a handful of straw on which the priest and the choir had stood. Then other peasants stooped and did the same. We believed that if this straw was mixed with cattle fodder, it would make the live-stock prolific and healthy.

All the time, I was edging cautiously nearer and nearer to Mr. Morianu. He stood a little apart from the others and watched them jostling and pushing. At last I reached him. I hurriedly took the note-book from under my sheepskin.

"It's my composition, sir," I said softly, handing it to him.

For a moment, Mr. Morianu did not seem to re-member anything about it.

"Which one?" he asked.

"The one about my dreams," I explained, and begged him to take it quickly, for fear Father might see it.

"You could have left it until next term," Mr. Morianu replied.

"I've nowhere to keep it at home," I explained. "My parents don't like me to write and study."

"Really," murmured Mr. Morianu to himself. He

looked at me with a peculiar expression. Then he stuffed the notebook into his coat pocket. I said good-bye and slipped back among the people still crowding by the river bank. My heart felt light and gay, like a bird in spring when the snow has melted and the fields and meadows are teeming with food.

My essay was safe with Mr. Morianu. Now everything would follow its course like a river in full spate, and not even Father could hold it back.

Chapter 6

IMPATIENCE

TWO MONTHS PASSED and I heard nothing more about my essay.

I had gone to school full of expectation the first morning after the Christmas holiday. I thought that as soon as Mr. Morianu came into the classroom he would call me to him and say something to me. But nothing happened at all, that day or the ones that followed.

In the afternoons, as I sat over my sewing at home, I could think of nothing but the composition I had written. Tomorrow, I thought; he will say something to me tomorrow, and then I shall find out what it's all about. I tried to imagine the very words Mr. Morianu would use. "That was a wonderful composition you wrote, Annuzza," or "You

must be a poet deep down inside you." That was
the kind of thing he was bound to say, I thought
confidently in those first few weeks.

But as time elapsed, I lost heart, and became
more and more depressed. There were times when
I felt convinced that I had not written a single
intelligible sentence in the whole essay.

Mother always told us not to pester God with
petty wishes in church, but all the same, I used to
finish every Paternoster with the plea that the
teacher would say something nice to me about my
essay. I prayed for it every Sunday. I even promised myself that if I were the first person to arrive
in church and stayed until the last, I should
hear something definite the following week.

If anyone else had known about it, they would
have laughed at me and, in a way, I knew myself
that it was all nonsense. But another part of me
believed in it firmly and although I waited
feverishly week after week for Sunday to come
round, I was never the first.

One Sunday I stole from the house a whole
hour before the service was due to start. When I
reached the church, the gate was still locked.

So I ran down the road toward the river. The
cross of ice had long since melted and the willow
bushes along the bank were covered with glittering rime. They looked as if they had been turned
to stone and would never bear green leaves again.

I do not know how long I stayed down by the

river, but suddenly I heard the church bells ring. Bunika always said that the bells were to warn people to come to church, but I never thought of them as threatening. To me they were always inviting.

When I reached the church, the gate was wide open, but I was relieved to see that the square in front was empty and that there was no one coming along the road yet. I made the sign of the cross and went inside. For a second, I thought that I was alone. Then I saw a figure kneeling in front of the altar. It was Barba, a woman from one of the farms high up in the mountains. Once again, someone else had got there first.

The only one who knew about my misery was Kuza. Every now and then she would make me a present of a new candle, and she often comforted me. That morning, we walked back to the farm side by side. She was much taller than I and just then she looked so lovely that I could hardly keep my eyes off her. Her cheeks were glowing from the cold and her eyes shone, and I was a little jealous.

Suddenly she put her arm round my shoulders and it felt as warm as an extra fur.

"You know, Annuzza," she said, "if you want a thing badly, you have to go on wishing hard for it, every day and every hour. Then it may come true, perhaps. . . ."

She spoke softly as if she were talking to herself. I had never heard her speak like that before.

For a second I laid my head on her shoulder. "I'll try," I said. "You're so nice to me."

Then the moment passed and we went on in our usual way through the winter morning, not at all as if we had, for an instant, been closer to each other than ever before.

From far away, I saw a dark figure standing near our gate. I seized Kuza by the arm. "Look! There's someone there!" I said, pointing in the direction of the farm.

"He looks like a stranger," declared Kuza. "He's wearing a dark coat and a hat."

"Perhaps it's the gentleman from the city," I said, in an excited voice, and started to run.

Kuza kept up with me. "You're always running!" she cried as we got nearer the gate. "You see! It's only the teacher."

"Yes, it's only the teacher," I echoed, but in my mind I added, perhaps he's bringing my essay back. Then I laughed at my own foolishness. He would never do that on a Sunday. He would have waited until school next day. In any case, Mr. Morianu knew that I had written it in secret, without my parents' knowledge.

By then I could make him out clearly, standing in the middle of the path. In his black coat, he stood outlined in the sunlight like a solitary tree trunk. My parents, who were following more slowly with Bunika and Puiu, had only reached the farm next door.

"There you are!" Mr. Morianu called to the two of us. "I've been waiting quite some time. Perhaps we can go on to the veranda until your parents come. It will be warmer there."

"No, it isn't," I told him. "The wind comes tearing round the corners as if it were playing catch."

Mr. Morianu laughed. "Maybe we could join in."

"Were you coming to see us, sir?" asked Kuza.

"Did you think I was waiting for Father Stanescu?" countered Mr. Morianu.

I had never seen him in such a jolly mood. He went on joking as we reached the veranda.

"You were quite right, Annuzza. The wind is really trying to bite its own tail."

When the rest of the family came in sight, Mr. Morianu went to meet them. As Father caught sight of him, he made a face as if someone had stuffed his pipe with sawdust.

I could not make out what Mr. Morianu was telling Father and Mother, but the astonishment on their faces showed me that it was something quite out of the ordinary.

"With pleasure, Mrs. Burda, with pleasure," I heard the teacher say and he followed Mother into the parlor. Father brought up the rear, scowling. Mother made a sign to us to go into the kitchen.

Bunika was already sitting in her own place on the settle below the icon. "The clouds are playing sadly," she muttered. That was her expression for stormy weather, but judging by the way she nodded her head in the direction of the parlor, she meant the tone of Father's voice.

Kuza knelt before the stove and started to make up the fire.

"Why are you trembling so?" Bunika asked me. "You're shivering like a horse that's been left standing too long in the cold."

"She's frightened!" Puiu chipped in. "She thinks the teacher's come to say she can't go to school any more." He emphasized his words with a sadistic grin. He always grinned that way when he thought that I was in for some punishment.

I turned away to avoid his expression. He was right. I was terribly afraid.

I started counting in my head — counting up to sixty over and over again. Every sixty meant another minute had gone, but I was incapable of putting the minutes together and I had no idea how long it was before I heard voices in the passage. Then the teacher's footsteps creaked over the veranda and crunched their way over the newly fallen snow.

"He can go to the Devil!" I heard Father say in a loud voice.

"Hush! You mustn't swear on the Lord's Day!" Mother tried to calm him down.

Then they both came into the kitchen. I made an effort to hide my trembling.

"He was there a long time," remarked Bunika, reproachfully. You could tell that she thought some explanation was due her.

"And he talked a lot of rubbish," growled Father, in a bad temper, it seemed. His pipe had gone out.

I was feverish. If only Mother would say something! But she just sat down at the table on the settle next to Bunika.

Puiu took the glass ball down from its shelf and began to play with it.

"Put that down!" Father shouted at him.

"What did the teacher want?" It was Kuza who dared to ask the question. Her voice was soft and lilting like a bird fluttering gently through the room.

Mother looked up. "He wants to send Annuzza away."

"Me? Where?" I pressed my fingers together until they bent.

"He wants her to go to the town. According to him, Annuzza is his best pupil and she has written a very good essay for him. If she passes an exam, she can get a free place at the high school in the city, the Lyceul Orthodox," Mother explained.

She spoke very calmly, but I think that she too was excited and even, perhaps, a little proud of me.

"Fiddlesticks," cried Father. "She's not going to study and she's not going to take any exams. Annuzza will stay here on the farm, where she belongs."

"We'll see about that," said Mother.

I could have hugged her. My thoughts went chasing round my head like the wind on the veranda. The stranger in the sleigh . . . the essay . . . the exam . . . the city . . . studying, studying. . . .

"The old folks always have to stay behind," said Bunika, as if to herself.

I hardly heard her. I had no idea what I should have to do for the exam, but it did not occur to me then that I might find it difficult. I wanted to cheer and sing and shout for joy, but I just stood there in front of the hearth, staring at the flames.

So it can be a good thing after all to pray, and to dream. . . .

Chapter 7

GRANDMOTHER'S TREASURE

I HAD SIX MONTHS before the exam took place in the autumn. If I got through, I should go as a boarder to the high school.

Mr. Morianu told me all about it and he gave me several books that he had brought for me from the city. I had to get down to it and study them, but that was not so easy. I just did not know when and where I could do it.

Father was always watching me with a set face to see that I worked hard at my tablecloths. By the time evening came and I lit my candle and got out the books, which I had hidden at the bottom of my clothes chest, my eyes were practically closing, I was so tired.

Kuza and I got on better than ever, but there was nothing she could do to help me. My parents never referred to the examination. I had hoped that Mother would stand up for me, but she probably couldn't because of Father.

Shortly before Easter, Mother sold the four tablecloths and brought back two laying hens from the market. Father prodded them all over.

"We'll see if one of them turns out to be a Mikuza," he said gruffly, and that was all.

Don't be silly, I told myself. You didn't really expect a few kind words of recognition and forgiveness, now did you?

I went out of the kitchen on to the veranda and as I looked up into the sky I watched the sun trying to push the clouds away. There were clouds in my life too, I thought, clouds that would not be pushed aside, either. There were so many things I had never even heard of in those thick books the teacher had given me. It seemed impossible to learn them all for the autumn.

I took a deep breath. The air smelled of spring. The lilac along the fence was heavy with thick white clusters. In the yard, Kuza was picking over the sheep shearings. As she did so, her body swayed like corn in the wind and she was singing. The song which reached me through the still afternoon was a *doina,* a lament. I listened to the words which I had never heard before.

Doina, doina, loud lamenting, how you
    sweeten all my days,
Doina, doina, silent sorrow, how you stab me
    to the heart.
Sweet yet bitter, sing your loudest
Or my heart will surely die....

It had never occurred to me before that Kuza
might be sad or have a private grief of her own. I
forgot my own cares and ran to her.

"What is wrong, Kuza?" I asked.

Kuza looked up at me in surprise, although her
fingers did not stop tugging at the earth-brown
tufts of wool.

"What do you mean?" she replied. "There's
nothing wrong. Why should there be?" Her eyes
shone as they always did.

I had forgotten for the moment that village
people were fond of singing these mournful laments, even when they weren't feeling sad at all.

I sat down on the ground near Kuza. The earth
was sprinkled with pale green shoots of young
grass.

"You are the one who's miserable," said Kuza.
"You look as if you'd like to cry."

I did not answer at once. Slowly my fingers
smoothed the tender blades.

"I'm afraid that I shan't get through the exam,"
I said at last. "Every single one of the books I have

to learn is thicker than our Bible. And Father told me yesterday that he expects me to work in the fields this summer like one of the hands."

"The fields are pretty big," said Kuza. "You'll find somewhere to read where Father won't find you."

"Oh, Kuza," I cried. "Of course! I can study in the maize field!"

As the spring days rushed by into summer and summer into autumn, the crops would grow and make me a secret shelter of yellow stems and green leaves. I could be alone among the maize.

Time passed. The books, which I had thought of at first as alien and sealed, gradually opened their pages for me. Their bindings grew faded and shabby from long hours out of doors in the wind and the sun. Fine sand drifted through the air in the hot noon and settled between the pages, but I did not mind. I was only glad that Father did not find out what I was doing.

Several times a week Mr. Morianu reminded me of the examination. "Don't let me down, Annuzza," he said sternly every time.

As the day of the examination drew nearer, I got more and more agitated. My head felt crammed full of the things in my books, like the blackboard in our classroom when Mr. Morianu had covered it with sentences for us to copy. Sometimes I was afraid that a damp sponge would descend and wipe away everything that I had learned, and I wondered if it might be better not to sit for the exam after all.

After school, I used to steal away to the maize field for an hour or two. The corn was ripening and day by day the sweet sap swelled the cobs beneath their ribbed leaves.

The examination was fixed for two weeks after the maize harvest. This year, at last, I should be there for the dance, the *klaka*. My thoughts and my dreams forked upward like the branches of a tree. They raced shoulder to shoulder, one of them preoccupied with the *klaka*, the other with the examination.

It was one warm afternoon after school. I lay in the field as I had done at this time last year, and once again I was daydreaming. I quite forgot the books in my satchel. My eyes were closed and I was thinking about the *klaka* next day and the dancing and singing there would be. It was exactly twelve months since the buzzard had killed Mikuza. Then I had been sent up into the mountains to see Drago, and I had caught a glimpse of a world that had been unknown to me before. What would happen now? This might be the first and the last *klaka* I would go to as a village child, and it aggravated me to think that I still did not possess an embroidered *katrinza* or beads to go around my neck. I should look plain and ugly, I felt sure.

All at once I heard a rustling through the thick

corn. It could not be the wind, for there was no breeze. I sat up to listen. There it was again. I hid my satchel hastily under a broad pumpkin leaf. Then I jumped to my feet. I could see something dark moving among the pale stems. I heard a voice calling my name. It was Kuza.

"I'm here!" I called. "Here!"

"Come home quickly," Kuza shouted back. "Mother's looking for you!"

I picked up my satchel and ran back to the farm with Kuza.

Mother was in the kitchen and she looked at me crossly.

"There's some *mamaliga* for you on the stove. We've all had our dinner. Father's very angry with you."

Oh, if only he didn't punish me and stop me from going to the *klaka*. I was horribly afraid.

"Eat your dinner quickly and you'd better have a wash," said Mother brusquely. "Then go round to the neighbors and tell them that we'll be cutting the maize tomorrow and invite them to come to the *klaka* in the evening."

"Yes," I answered. I was dying to ask her if it would be all right for me to come too for the first time in my life, but I did not dare. I was scared that she would ask me where I had been hiding since school had closed.

"Come along, Kuza. We've work to do," said Mother, and she trudged heavily out of the house.

I found what was left of the *mamaliga* on the polished stove. We used to eat it nearly every day, and I liked it. I liked it better than anything else Mother cooked: potatoes, vegetables, eggs, bacon, or even meat. *Mamaliga* reminded me of the maize field, of the taste of ripe corn, and of the dolls I used to make out of the empty cobs.

On the settle behind the table sat Bunika. I took the shallow dish in which the food stood, poured some sour cream over it, and cut a slice of curd cheese. Then I sat down by Bunika's side.

"I suppose you were playing, as usual?" said Bunika, poking two fingers under the skimpy black headscarf she wore, so that I could see a wisp of gray hair above her wrinkled forehead.

"No," I answered, "I was seeing to the cows." I started eating quickly to avoid looking her in the face.

Bunika was as old as the beech tree in the courtyard and her face was as wrinkled as its bark. She did not know exactly how old she was. Sometimes she said she was ninety, sometimes ninety-five. She could even have been a hundred. In our village people lived to a good old age, and Bunika was one of the oldest. Her eyes looked as wise as if they had seen the whole world and lived through several lifetimes. Or perhaps it was just that she had watched so many good harvests and had also survived plenty of bad ones.

I knew that she could tell just by looking at me that I had been nowhere near the cows.

"Puiu is with the cows," she muttered.

"No, he's in the yard," I retorted.

"Father's in such a bad temper, he'll drink too much out in the fields," she said.

"Father drinks too much even when he isn't angry," put in Puiu from the kitchen door, which was open. I had not heard him come in.

Bunika shrugged her shoulders and reached out for a black earthenware pitcher with a colored pattern round it, which had been standing near her on the bench. She turned it upside down and a heap of coins tumbled out on to the table. Then she began to count them and put them back into the jug, one by one.

My parents had to give Bunika one tenth of all they got for the farm's produce — each pound of butter and cheese, every single egg, everything they grew and sold. The money was her tithe, her treasure. She counted it over every day at dinner time, and she watched over it like a miser and hid the jug away, no one knew where.

Puiu came over to the table and the two of us watched Bunika's hands, fascinated. Her crooked fingers and gnarled skin reminded me of the roots of a tree. I could not help admiring the skill with which she handled the coins and tossed them back into the jug.

Bunika was the one who ruled our house and farm and fields. The rest of us — Father, Mother, Kuza, and I — did the work, but it was Bunika who gave the orders and you could tell how things were faring with us from her face, just as you can tell the weather by the flight of the swallows. It was not only on our farm that a Bunika ruled the roost. The same thing happened in every house in the village where there was a grandmother alive still.

As I finished the last spoonful of *mamaliga*, I saw that the wide sleeves of her linen blouse had caught two silver coins and swept them to the edge of the table. One of them, a five-*lei* piece, tipped up and rolled silently on to the kitchen floor which was made of trodden clay. Bunika did not notice it. She went on counting stolidly.

I glanced at Puiu. His face was a blank and I could not tell whether or not he had seen the coin fall. Five *lei*, I thought: you could buy a colored necklace at Moishe's for that. I had never possessed so much money in my life. For five *lei*, I could buy a necklace of red and green and yellow beads to wear at my first *klaka* and at the examination, too.

I looked at the floor warily. There lay the coin, round and silver and irresistible. It was only a few inches from my toes, quite close to the table leg.

I looked at Bunika, then back at Puiu. Bit by bit I slid my bare foot to the right until I could feel the cold metal pressing against the skin. With a slight jerk I worked the coin toward me and then sat quite still again.

Puiu was looking at me. Had he seen? My heart thumped.

I pushed a spoon off the table with my elbow and it fell to the ground with a clatter. I bent down quickly to pick up the spoon and the money with it. As I clutched it, I could feel the blood mounting to my cheeks.

I had the five-*lei* piece. It was not mine, but I had it.

"You had better go now, Annuzza," said Bunika. "A farm will never thrive where the master drinks and the children are idle and tell lies and the mistress has to spend half the day calling them. Don't go back to the cows. Go and tell the neighbors that the maize is ripe."

That was a long speech for Bunika. She did not often say so much at a time. Her voice was low and she did not look up from her counting. All the same, I did not miss a word, and I understood what she left unspoken too.

Bunika had not missed the coin. It burned my hand like a glowing coal. I felt nervous, but I was pleased too.

"Well? Aren't you off yet?" muttered Bunika.

I got up and took the empty dish back to the hearth, pressing the money against the handle. With my back to the table I slid the coin into my sleeve. Then I turned and watched Bunika putting the last of the money into the jug. She chalked a white sign on the black clay. It was not a number nor yet a letter, for Bunika could not write, but it must have been a special mark that she had made up and only she understood.

"Don't stand there idling, Puiu. Go and tend the cattle."

As she spoke, she lifted her hand with a characteristic gesture that reminded me of a gust of wind through the corn, and she shooed Puiu out of the kitchen. I watched him, but he gave no indication that he had seen me pick up the money from under the table. He turned round at the veranda and pulled a cheeky face. Then I saw him take the stick, which he had carved himself, and run off, barefoot, with quick jerky footsteps, to the fields.

As soon as Puiu had gone, I left the kitchen without another glance at Bunika. A broad beam of light from the parlor window fell on the homemade carpet and I ran across it to the door of the room I had shared with Kuza for the last two years.

I sat down on her bed. Our room was hardly wider than the footpath between the fields leading to the farm. There were two beds, bunk fashion, against one wall. Along the opposite wall were our two clothes chests. Father had painted a red "A" between the designs on the lid of one of the chests and a blue "K" on the other one. My chest was half-empty and I could easily push it over to the window in the evening when I wanted to read by moonlight. Kuza's was heavy by comparison and filled to the brim with white blouses and skirts, belts, and beads, and sleeveless lambskin jackets heavy with multicolored embroidery. In my eyes Kuza was rich, nearly as rich as Father Stanescu.

I put my hand up my sleeve and took out the coin. I felt rich too, rich enough to buy some beads at any rate. But what if Bunika noticed that she was five *lei* short when she counted her hoard again at dinner time next day? Perhaps Puiu had seen me after all and was waiting to give me away later. My hands grew clammy with fear. You never knew with Puiu. It would mean the end of everything — the *klaka* and the new life that the examination promised for me. Probably I should not even be allowed to go into the town to sit for it. . . .

Don't worry, I told myself. Tomorrow I would wait until Bunika had counted her money and if she said nothing, then it would be safe to go along to Moishe and buy myself those beads for the five *lei*. My mind was made up.

Slowly I opened the lid of my chest and took out the long girdle that Mother had woven for me last winter to wear on Sundays. She had embroidered it with silk in blue and red and yellow, our national colors.

Near Kuza's bed hung her little mirror. I un-hooked it and stood it on the window sill to see myself better. I wound the girdle several times round my waist so that the ends hung down and made my skirt seem less plain. I looked all right to go round to the neighbors, I decided.

For safety, I put the silver coin in the little purse that was worked into the back of the belt. I could feel its hard round outline distinctly when I put my hand there. It's mine, I told myself.

The door from the parlor into the passage was kept locked on weekdays, and I did not want to go through the kitchen past Bunika again. So I decided to get out through the bedroom window into the yard. Kuza used to keep her treasures on the window sill. There was a photograph of Mihai in uniform. Mihai was Kuza's husband-to-be and although they were not yet engaged, Mihai had sent her a snapshot from the town where he was stationed. Among the painted Easter eggs on a wooden platter was a tattered Easter card on which was printed: "Christ is risen!" Below, added in pencil, was: "Truly, He is risen! Mihai."

We seldom received letters on the farm, so this postcard from the town had caused quite a sensa-tion. For a long time Kuza carried it about all day tucked in her belt, and she read it to herself every evening before she went to sleep.

I put the dish and photograph carefully to one side, climbed on to the sill, opened one side of the casement and jumped. There was Mother chopping cabbage on a big square board. It was for stuffing yeast cakes for the next day's *klaka*. She looked up and said curtly, "Only thieves climb through windows, Annuzza."

That was all, but it was enough to make my hand dart to the coin in my belt, to make me feel nervous and ashamed of myself.

I wondered if it mightn't be best after all to slip back into the kitchen and leave the coin on the floor there. But then I should have no beads to wear for the dance.

"Have you had a wash yet?" asked Mother.

"Yes . . . no, I mean I'm just going to," I stammered.

Mother shook her head. "You don't come when I call you, and when I tell you to do a thing, you don't get on with it," she said. "You're hopeless, Annuzza."

I turned and ran round the house toward the well, and Mother's words went with me too. "You're hopeless, Annuzza." Could Mother be right? But still, I had written a good essay, and that time, a year ago, I really had closed the door to the poultry-run. I wanted to be a success in life. Father, Mother, Bunika, they should all be proud of me. I wanted to get through the exam and I intended to be more than just a peasant's wife when I grew up. I might be a teacher or I might marry one.

Tomorrow I would ask the teacher what my chances were of getting through. He was cleverer even than Father Stanescu and could do more than read and write and count. He had been to Bucharest once and he had seen the place where the Danube flows into the Black Sea. He was a widely traveled man. I thought that Mr. Morianu would be sure to know the answer to my question and then, perhaps, I should lose my terror of the ordeal.

These things went round my head as I washed myself over the rain-butt. Then I set out for the village, wondering if Moishe had a cheap necklace on display in the narrow glass showcase outside his house. I could at least take a look and see. I only wanted to have a look.

Tomorrow I would not hide myself away in the fields to study and I would never take five *lei* again. It's just this once, dear God, I promise, just this time.

Soon the broad highway lay before me. It had not rained for several days and at every step my bare feet kicked up a light cloud of yellow dust.

The houses to the left and right were yellow or pink, pale blue or a delicate green. In the light of the sun, they looked as pretty as young girls. Hardly any peasants lived in these houses. Most of them belonged to woodcutters or craftsmen and their children played on the wooden doorsteps every day. The boys would be carving or making pots, the nimble fingers of the girls embroidering white linen for shirts and blouses.

I knew all the children. We helped in the fields, and we played together, and we all went to the same school.

"Good day, Annuzza!" they called to me from all sides as I passed them.

"*Buna zuia, buna zuia!*" I called back.

Moishe's house had two stories like the priest's, and it looked very imposing and rich by the side of the low-built cottages of the other villagers. It was made of stone and distempered white. You could buy anything at Moishe's. Father said that he was a good business man and earned more money than anyone else in the whole village. But he would also give goods on credit. He wrote the amount down and when the debt was large enough, he would take a slice of land instead of the cash.

There was a showcase on the wall near the entrance to the shop and although the glass was dull and grimy, the things behind it seemed beautiful to me. There were a pair of white gloves, long pendant earrings, two pipes, wooden picture frames in assorted sizes, a pair of black high-heeled shoes like Kuza's, and three necklaces. One was white, one was red, and the other was mixed. I moved my head from side to side a little so that the brightly colored beads gleamed and flashed, catching first the shadow and then the sunlight.

My hand traveled up to my bare neck. I could see it reflected in the glass. Tomorrow there would be beads there. It was the colored necklace I wanted, the prettiest of all in my opinion. If I closed my eyes, I could imagine that it was mine already. I had seen my beads and they were the ones I was going to buy.

All the neighbors would come next day, and I should be there too, with a necklace of my own. What a day to look forward to! It was very nearly as important as taking my examination.

Chapter 8

THE NECKLACE

WE HAD BEEN WORKING in the maize field since six that morning. Except for Bunika, the whole family was there, as well as our two farm-hands and many of our neighbors, dark figures against the bright yellow stalks of maize. Now the sun was high overhead. With even movements we cut the cobs and let them fall to the earth.

Maria Petrescu was busy by my side.

"Will you be allowed to go to the *klaka*?" Maria asked.

"Yes," I answered.

"Next year I can go too," declared Maria, who was only just eleven.

"That's a whole winter to wait and another harvest away," said I.

Most of the neighbors had brought their children to help. Even Marcel, the Burgomaster's son, had come. We collected the cobs as they were cut and carried them to our farm cart, which stood on the path already yoked. Father had placed boards between the slats, so that the corn would not fall through.

As I was passing Mother with my arms full, she said, "That's the fourth cartload, Annuzza. Go back to the farm with Father and bring the dinner. It's time to eat."

"Yes, Mother," I said.

I had nearly reached the cart when I saw Father coming from the far side of the field, plodding along heavily. He's been drinking again, I thought. At supper the night before, he had not said a single word to me, good or bad. He did not even look at me.

"What do you want, Annuzza?" he asked testily.

"I have to go with you to get the dinner," I replied.

"Nothing else?" said Father, looking at me. His breath smelled of liquor and there were little wrinkles round his eyes. His face was sunburned and his linen smock, which hung loose to his hips, was wet from the strenuous work in the warm midday sun.

"Well," I said, "I'm sorry about yesterday. . . ." It was never easy to apologize to Father.

"We'll let it pass, this time," said Father. "After all, it's the harvest today."

He's forgiven me, I thought, and for sheer joy, I forgot that my arms were full of cobs. They fell unheeded to the ground and I seized Father's hand to kiss it, which is the custom with us when we want to thank our parents. But Father pulled his hand away roughly and laid it on my head. It felt as heavy as the basket of cheese and eggs that Mother sometimes carried on her head to market.

"There, there — it doesn't matter," and Father swung himself up on to the driving seat of the cart, which was just a narrow board. I sat by his side.

"Hi, there, children! Puiu, Maria, Marcel!" called Father. "You can come along too and help us to unload."

Then he turned back again and took the reins. He made a clicking noise with his tongue and Huzu, our cart-horse, started off at a trot. Puiu and the other two ran by the side of the cart. The wheels sometimes stumbled into a rut so that now and again a few of the cobs were spilled into the road. Puiu bent down to pick them up and throw them back. One of the cobs struck Father in the back.

"Hey, there!" cried Father, turning around. "That hurt! But not as much as it would if I threw it back!" And he roared with laughter.

Father was in a good mood, I thought. It must

have been the thought of the *klaka*, the dancing, the feasting, and lots to drink. I had seldom seen him like that. Now the most important thing was to find out if Bunika had missed the five *lei*. I thought that she might have counted her hoard already.

When the farm came into sight, I saw the great stack of corncobs lying in front of the house. It grew with every cartload, and in two or three hours it would be quite a mountain. I remembered from previous years that when the whole crop had been cut, only the roof of the house could be seen from the road.

Father led Huzu close in and he and I both jumped down. He pulled the boards away and most of the maize rolled through the slats on to the ground. Puiu, Maria, and Marcel climbed up on to the cart and threw the rest of the cobs on to the pale green hillock, swinging them with great sweeps of their arms as if they were mowing the ripe corn.

"Get the dinner, Annuzza," Father ordered me. "We're going straight back."

I stepped into the kitchen where Bunika was sitting in her usual place. "Well?" she said. "Getting the dinner?"

I nodded in silence. She examined me so intently that her eyes seemed tinier than ever. By her side on the bench was the black pitcher. Had she counted it yet, I wondered. My heart was beating wildly, like the sparrows' wings as they flutter away in swarms when you disturb them in the ripe cornfields. I had to think of something to ask her and try to tell from her answer if she knew.

"Anything wrong, Bunika?" I asked.

"You should all think more about work and less about food," she mumbled. She said no word about the five *lei*, at least not yet.

I got the dishes together and took the smooth wooden spoons from the table drawer, but I kept watching Bunika out of the corner of my eye.

I saw her feel in her girdle and take a piece of chalk from it. Then she made her secret mark on the jug as she did every day when she had finished counting. She'd counted it then, and she hadn't noticed! I could buy my beads! My head whirled. I wanted to rush out and shout aloud. "I can buy my beads!"

I carried the pots quickly, one after the other, out to the cart which had been cleared by now, and I placed the food carefully in the middle. Father was nowhere to be seen.

"Where's Father?" I asked Puiu, who was sitting on the heap of corn with Maria and Marcel.

"He went round to the back," said Puiu. "Let's have a game till he's ready."

Puiu meant the special game we played every year as the maize was stacked. Although I did not feel like playing, I thought that if I didn't join in, Puiu might wonder why. So I climbed on to "our"

mountain and the dry green leaves which sheathe
the cobs rustled like the woods in autumn.

Puiu called out. "Let's slide down. One, two,
three, off!"

The four of us had been sitting back to back at
the top of the stack and as Puiu gave the word,
we all set off in different directions. The leaves
were smooth and the idea was to see who would
be the first to reach the ground. From my side, I
could see Maria throwing her weight forward as
hard as she could and calling "Hi!" Until this year,
I had always been keen to win, but today I didn't
care a bit. I kept thinking of my beads and how I
could get away without being seen, so that I could
slip down to Moishe's.

"I've won!" shouted Puiu and he was so excited
that his voice squeaked.

"No, I was first!" contradicted Maria.

"No quarreling now. It's as bad as burnt *mamaliga*," said Father, who had come on the scene
unobserved. "Let's try the jumping game instead.
I'll be umpire and then there'll be no arguing
afterwards."

Father meant the other game we played from the
maize stack, which was much harder than sliding.
At once Puiu scrambled up to the top of the hillock
again. He crouched down, crossed his arms behind
his back, and jumped. Light as a feather he soared
through the air and landed upright on the veranda.

"Now you, Maria," Father told her and clapped

his hands. His eyes flashed as if he were enjoying himself.

But Maria was not as successful as Puiu. She touched one of the wooden posts as she landed and Father shook his head. "No good," he said.

Marcel did no better, for he turned to look at me as he jumped, with the result that he collided with the veranda rail and sat down with a bump, a very poor effort. I did not really want to play, but I climbed up and I landed in the yard, at least half a yard short of the veranda.

"What's the matter with you?" Father asked me. Then he added, "Well, it can't be helped. Puiu has won. He can ride by my side on the way back." Father whisked Puiu into the air as if he were as light as a corncob and seated him on his shoulders. I had seldom seen Father in such high spirits. Perhaps it was because he was convinced that I should not get through my exam.

As I walked back to the field by the side of the cart, I realized that a year before I should have been most upset at not winning any of the games. Now I did not care. I did not even mind giving up my place near Father to Puiu. It was far more important that I should go and buy my beads, that I should dance the *hora* as lightly as Kuza when the *klaka* started, and that I should get through my exam.

It was several hours later, when the dinner had long since been eaten and the last of the corn had been cut in the farthest corner of the field, that I edged my way between the naked stalks. Unfortunately Marcel kept close by my side. He wanted me to promise him that I would sit near him at the *klaka* and that I would dance with him later. What would he say if he knew about my going away to school?

I kicked a pebble to one side impatiently. Why couldn't I shake him off? I had to go to Moishe's.

"I'll tell you what," I said. "Let's play hide-and-seek in the field."

"Will you dance with me later if I do?" he asked.

"Yes, yes," I said. If only I could slip away unnoticed. "You hide first and I'll be it."

Marcel nodded. We counted three together. "But you mustn't look. Close your eyes!" he called.

I heard the pumpkin leaves rustling; then all was quiet. Cautiously I looked around. There was no one in sight. I cut across the field and ran toward the village. Kuza was right. I could not walk slowly these days, not to save my life. Marcel might be cross if I didn't look for him. Oh well, I'd just say that I couldn't find him. I kept looking back, but no one seemed to have noticed that I had gone.

There was not much time. The sunflowers at the edge of the fields were bowing their heads toward the setting sun and it was getting late. Soon the neighbors would be going home to change for the *klaka* and I had to be home before they got back.

But when I finally stood outside the shop door, I hesitated. Until today, I had never thought twice about going into the little shop on various errands for Mother, to buy salt or sugar or spices. Today was different, though. The five *lei* pressed against me. Suppose Moishe asked me where I had gotten the money? Wouldn't it be better to go home? But it was too late. Without thinking, I had pushed the door open and the shop bell shrilled. I jumped. It had never startled me before, but now I stood petrified in the doorway. I thought suddenly of all my deceptions of the past few months. What would happen if someone who knew me came into the shop while I was being served?

From behind the counter a spry little figure emerged. "Kindly close the door," he called out to me. "Kindly step inside."

I bit back my laughter. I always wanted to laugh at the way Moishe looked and the way he talked. With every step he took, he swayed from side to side like an outsized pendulum and as he spoke his pointed beard bobbed up and down. He kept pulling at it too, just as Mother pulled the dough when she was making yeast cakes. Moishe spoke Romanian very quaintly and very fast, and once he had started he hardly paused for breath.

I closed the door and the bell stopped, but I could still hear it in my ears.

"And what would the young lady like?" asked Moishe.

I couldn't think why he said "young lady" to me. He had never done it before. Surely he knew who I was, just Annuzza Burda, one of the village children. He had always addressed me as a little girl before. It was true that I had not been in his shop for several weeks but had I really changed in so short a time? I made myself a bit taller.

"I'd . . . I'd like some beads," I said at last.

"Ah . . . beads . . . let me see," repeated Moishe, as if I had voiced some outlandish request. "Would the lady like beads for her neck or for her arms? Or for her ears perhaps?"

"I want a necklace," I said quickly.

"Oh, we have so many necklaces. Like grains of sand, we have so many. There isn't a shop in the city with such a wonderful selection of beads." He ran to a low glass case and came back to the counter with his left arm festooned in necklaces to the elbow. There were long ones and short ones, colored and white, dull and shining, and different kinds of *salbas,* which are made of coins and very popular with peasant girls. They jingled and jangled like a peal of bells.

Moishe spread them all out before me, and if you could credit all he said, each one was a unique specimen at a bargain price. The words came tumbling out one after the other like a shower of grain when a sack is split. He tried them on in turn, and again I had to laugh inside. I couldn't help it. Moishe, with beads on!

"If the young lady wears Moishe's necklace, she will be the prettiest girl at the dance," he kept repeating.

I did not like any of them as much as the one in the glass case outside, but I hesitated to say so for fear he might be offended. I had never bought any beads before.

"The young lady should buy a *salba*. It's as good as cash. It's practically real silver," he rattled on.

I shook my head.

"I should like to buy the colored one in the glass case outside," I said hastily.

"That one? There must be some mistake. Those are very cheap, very shoddy. They are only four and a half *lei*."

"That's the one," I assured him.

Moishe looked up at me, hurt. With a contemptuous flourish he swept the other necklaces to one side, and then he brought me the one from the case near the door. Oh, it was lovely! The colors shone like the rainbow. And it cost only four and a half *lei!*

I paid him in a hurry and put the beads and the change in my girdle.

"*Buna seara*," I said, and made for the door.

"*Buna seara*," said Moishe. "I hope the young lady will honor me with her custom again," and as he said it, he made a reluctant little bow. I knew that for grander customers he bowed several times and very low, but that did not worry me.

I had the beads, the shining, glittering beads. All the way home I kept fingering the small hard shapes through the thickness of my girdle.

I conveniently forgot that I had bought them with Bunika's money. Indeed, I refused to think about it. But it was not long before it was brought home to me.

Chapter 9

THE HARVEST DANCE

I HAD CHANGED MY CLOTHES and I was standing in the bedroom in front of Kuza's mirror. It was a pity it was so small that I could see only a bit of me at a time. I had rubbed a little melted lard into my hair and it shone like black silk. My colored girdle hung down over my *katrinza* and then I tried the necklace on, this way and that. I liked it best with the beads lying over the opening of my blouse. They went twice round my neck and they felt like a warm hand where they touched my skin. They made me look almost pretty, I thought, and that delighted me.

I could hear footsteps in the passage and on the veranda. The first guests had arrived. I would have to hurry.

But still I lingered, and catching up the edge of
my skirt, I twirled round in a circle so that the
heavy embroidery at the edge of my underskirt
showed. The beads tinkled a little as I whirled
round. I kept catching sight of myself in the little
mirror and I was still absorbed in my dance when
the door opened and Kuza came in. I stood still
where the candlelight fell on me and I looked at
her expectantly, wondering what she would say
to my beads.

"Are you ready?" she asked, glancing straight
past me into the mirror.

She had not noticed my string of beads! I was
not only disappointed, I was hurt. "Do look at me!"
I said, poking out my chin a little.

Kuza turned round and stared in silence. Surely
she had something to say, or was the necklace
so lovely that it took her breath away?

"Where did you get those beads?" I heard her
ask.

My hand flew to my neck. In my blind excitement, it had never occurred to me that anyone
would ask "Where did you get those beads?" What
could I say? Mother would ask me and so would
Father, and Bunika too. The question shattered
all my joy at a single blow.

Kuza pulled my hand away and felt the beads.
"They're new ones," she said. "Where did you get
them?" she insisted.

"I . . . I bought them," I hesitated.

"Where did you get the money?"

"I had some," I said defiantly. Why did she keep on at me so?

"Where did you get it from?" Kuza's questions pinned me down, and the room was so narrow that I could not slip past her and out through the door.

"It doesn't matter where I got it," I answered at last.

"Oh yes, it does," said Kuza obstinately. "Come on, now. Tell me."

"From . . . from Bunika."

"That's not true," declared Kuza and she shook her head so that her long silver earrings jingled.

"Yes, it is," I tried to defend myself.

"Bunika never gives money away," said Kuza curtly.

"I . . . I took it myself." My voice was very subdued. I bent my head and undid the clasp with tired hands.

"Annuzza," said Kuza, seizing me by the shoulders, "you stole it from Bunika. . . ."

I pushed her hands away and threw myself on her bed. I hid one hand under the pillow, still clutching the beads. My face was wet with tears. Kuza had told me clearly and bluntly what I had simply refused to admit to myself. I was a thief. I should never be able to wear the beads, that night or any other night, never.

Kuza sat down on the edge of the bed. Her hand

smoothed my hair. "Annuzza," she said, "you ought to be glad that I saw you before you went out there and got into trouble. If I were you, I'd go straight to Moishe now and ask him to let you have the money back."

I sobbed aloud. My beads . . .

"Don't cry, Annuzza. I've never thought much about these things before, but believe me, no beads in the world can ever be as precious as a clear conscience. You'd better let me have them."

My face was still buried in the pillow. Wearily I drew out my hand and let the beads trickle into Kuza's lap, slowly, one by one. I did not want to see them again. I did not want to go to the dance either. I wanted to stay in my room, alone. I had no beads now and instead of a pretty necklace I should have only my tears and a blotchy face.

Kuza lifted my head and wiped my cheeks with her wide sleeve. Through blurred eyes I saw her go to her chest and come back with a red necklace in her hands.

"You may wear this tonight. There! Now you can laugh again. Tomorrow I'll go and ask Moishe to take the other one back and you can slip the money into Bunika's jug."

As she spoke, she spun me round twice very quickly like a top. "Come on, Annuzza. Let me see you smile. You'll be able to buy plenty of beads when you are older. Only you must never steal again. Promise me."

"I promise you," I said slowly, and the promise was to myself too.

Then I followed Kuza through the parlor and the passage onto the veranda. It was a mercy that it was dark and the only illumination came from the moon and the stars. At least no one could tell that I had been crying.

Mother came toward us across the yard. "Where have you been?" she asked. "Everyone's here already."

Kuza put her arm round my shoulder. I could feel the warm pressure of her fingers. "I had to tidy myself up a bit," she declared, "and Annuzza waited for me."

"Hurry up then, they want to start," said Mother.

The people were sitting in a huge circle round the stack of corn. I could see Father, and I pushed farther along past him to an empty space on a bench. Voices hummed and there was laughter and joking.

"Forget about the beads," whispered Kuza to me. "See what a lovely night it is!" Her face was turned to the stars. Kuza was even lovelier than the clear autumn evening and so good-hearted, too. She was so kind and beautiful, it was no wonder I loved her so dearly. She had wound her braid around her head into a crown, with two glossy ribbons — a blue one and a red one — woven in and out of the fairness of her hair. I imagine

that I looked like a little black ant by her side, but
I was too grateful to her to feel jealous.

"You promised me something this afternoon." It
was Marcel. How grown up he looked in his
embroidered Sunday shirt, with its full sleeves. I
had quite forgotten my promise, so I had to close
in a little nearer to Kuza and make room for Marcel next to me. He sat down and we each reached
for a corncob without another word. Glancing
sideways, I saw a smile on Kuza's face. Was it
because of Marcel? I was not sure if she was laughing at us or if she was pleased that he wanted to
sit near me.

I looked around me. Kuza was right. It was a
lovely picture. The moon gleamed like a pale
lantern. In its mellow light the white-shirted figures
reminded me of puppets, or the straw scarecrows
Mother used to put in the fields to protect the
crops. Only their hands moved, deftly stripping
away the half-dried leaves and the shining brown
corn silk. When they had finished a cob, they
tossed it vigorously over one shoulder so that the
empty yellow corncobs gradually piled up into
an outer ring encircling us all.

I wondered if Mr. Morianu had come yet. He
had been invited as well as the Burgomaster.

"Are you looking for someone?" asked Marcel
on my left. His voice sounded angry, but I could
not guess why.

"I'm looking for the teacher," I answered.

"He's sitting over there near your father." There was a pause before he went on, "Is it true that you are going to the city to take an exam?"

I could feel my heart give an excited little jump. "How do you know?" I countered.

"I heard Mr. Morianu talking about it to your father," replied Marcel gruffly.

"Maybe," I said.

"Then you'll be leaving the village?" he continued.

"I might," I answered.

"Why didn't you tell me anything about it?" he persisted.

"Because I don't know if I'll pass or not. And Mother always tells us not to count our chickens before they are hatched." I tried to make a joke of it.

Marcel was not in the mood for joking. "Well — I hope you don't get through," he said hoarsely and jumped up.

Let him go then. He wanted me to fail. He's as hard and unsympathetic as Father, I thought.

Just then, two broad beams of light fell across the yard. Father had brought out the oil-lamps and hung them from the veranda posts. I saw Mother setting out yeast cakes on the kitchen table which had been carried out into the courtyard. A few of the men got up to fetch their musical instruments which they had left on the veranda.

Now that there was a lull in the feasting and

playing and dancing, perhaps I could have a word with the teacher. Father was in one corner of the yard, lighting a bonfire of brushwood. The flickering flames lit up the laughing figures, outlined against the heap of maize which was not quite so high now. In previous years I had watched the *klaka* secretly from the house, but now I could take part for the first time. Gradually all the aggravation I had felt about the beads began to fade.

"Well, Annuzza? Enjoying yourself?" Mother asked me as she passed with another tray of yeast cakes.

"Oh yes. It's lovely," I answered and jumped up.

The first *hora* was just beginning. This is a dance in which you make a great circle and put your arms on the shoulders of both your neighbors. The ones who were not dancing sat round and clapped their hands in time to the music. It's a beautiful dance, particularly by firelight. Above the clash of the cymbals, the sound of the flute and the *cobza*, the Burgomaster's violin yearned like the call of a bird.

I saw Mr. Morianu leaning against the garden fence not far from the bonfire, watching the next figure of the dance in which the circle breaks up into couples. I was just going up to him when Marcel barred my way. "Father says that they're going to play a *moldovenesca* next. Will you be my partner?" he asked and took my hand.

"I thought you had gone," I said, and tried to

pull my hand away, but he held it tight. "I've only come to claim the dance you promised me."

"But you're angry with me. Why do you want to dance with me?"

Marcel did not reply, nor was there any answer in his face. In the firelight it looked like an expressionless mask. His cool slanting eyes betrayed nothing. He spun me round in the fast rhythm of the dance until I was quite out of breath. Oh! It was fun dancing with Marcel!

My braid came unpinned and flew from side to side. When the music finally stopped, Marcel said, "All the same, even if you do go to the city, you'll come back one day."

"Never!" I replied defiantly and stamped my foot.

"Yes, you will," said Marcel brusquely, "and then we shall dance together again."

I wanted to call after him that I wouldn't dream of it, that I would never dance with him again because he was so beastly to me, but I was alone. Marcel had been swallowed up in the darkness of the gateway and vanished.

He's a boor, I thought passionately. He's a . . . a Hun! I'll show him though. If I get through that examination, I shall stay in the town for good.

"Well, well, Annuzza! You look as if you'd just had a ducking in the pond."

Mr. Morianu was standing near me and he gave me a searching look. I shook my head emphatically and pinned up my braid again. "No," I said, "it's nothing."

He turned to go, but I went with him.

"Please, sir, do you think I'll pass the exam?" I asked timidly.

"Are you nervous, Annuzza?"

"Yes, I am," I answered.

"Do you remember that Sunday, when the wind started biting its own tail as it blew round the veranda?"

I nodded.

"You'd better make sure that it doesn't happen to you," said Mr. Morianu. "Sometimes people can behave as foolishly as the wind. For instance, when we're afraid, we may hurt ourselves in sheer panic. Now if you keep cool and try to imagine that you are just having an ordinary test in your own classroom at school, you'll soon find the right answers, my girl."

"Do you really think so?"

"Of course I do," he said, and I could feel that his words were chosen to give me the confidence I lacked. But for all that, I did not think you could send fear packing as if you were chasing away a dog. Once the *klaka* was over, once the music was still and the neighbors had all gone home, I should have a whole long fortnight alone with my fear.

Chapter 10

THE EXAMINATION

KUZA TOOK THE BEADS BACK to Moishe for me, but he would give her only four *lei* for them. He said that once they had been worn, he could not sell them as new any more. I explained to Kuza that it left me a bit short and she made up the money for me, for she earned ten *lei* a month, doing housework for the Burgomaster's wife and for Mrs. Morianu. So the day after the *klaka* I was able to slip the money back into Bunika's jug without being seen.

I watched Bunika counting her tithe afterwards and she shook her head incredulously. She said nothing, but she was obviously pleased about something and in such a good mood that she sent Puiu to Moishe's to buy some boiled sweets. She gave us each one out of the little bag and put the rest away in her jug.

As I dropped the coin into the pitcher, my bad conscience vanished with it. I realized this when I found myself singing for the first time for days as Kuza and Puiu and I sat on the veranda, threading the husked corncobs on to a string for Father to hang round the roof. The house would look as if it were thickly fringed with yellow wax candles. In a few weeks, the corn would be dry and we could rasp off the grains and take them to the mill nearby to be ground. Did I really mean "we"? My thoughts strayed back to the town and I wondered if I would still be helping on the farm in a month or so.

Every day I tried to repeat to myself all that I had learned. I asked myself questions and I gave myself the right answers. But in spite of it, I was still diffident, for they might ask quite different questions in the actual test.

The days were growing shorter now. Neither Father nor Mother mentioned the exam. I knew how a bird must feel when the others had flown south and left it behind. I was on my own and there was no one to whom I could turn. I did not even dare to inquire how I should get to the town.

Two days before the examination was due, we were all sitting round the dinner table eating *mamaliga* and beans, when Mother said suddenly, "I shall need Huzu and the small wagon the day after tomorrow. The horse must be properly groomed, Burda."

"Why?" asked Father.

"I'm driving Annuzza into town — for the exam."

Kuza winked at me cheerfully and Puiu pulled a face. Bunika kept shaking her head. She always did when something displeased her. Father growled in an ill-humored voice. "Don't waste the journey at any rate. You might as well take the eggs and butter to market with you. You'll have to bring Annuzza back, in any case."

"Well, we'll see," said Mother.

I remembered that she had answered Father with those same words that Sunday months ago when the teacher came to our house. I could not swallow another bite, I was so full of joy and excitement and apprehension, for I did not know if the great day would bring about my triumphal departure from the village or a humiliating return.

A night can be as long as a journey without a goal. I lay in bed on the eve of the examination with my eyes open, staring at the whitewashed ceiling. From time to time I painted imaginary pictures in the dark with my finger: the hen-house, or Marcel's face; a long string of beads, or a flock of sheep up in the mountain pastures. Then I tried counting to myself. I kept thinking it must soon be morning, but when I heard the church clock strike, only another quarter hour had gone. I do not know for sure if I dropped off or not, but when the sun rose, I had the feeling that I had lain awake all night. My eyes were smarting and my feet felt heavy. I should have liked to stay in bed the whole day, but the door opened and Mother called, "Up with you, Annuzza! We'll be leaving in half an hour."

When I jumped out of bed, I saw that Kuza was awake. She propped herself up on one elbow and said, "You may wear my white blouse and the blue skirt from the chest. I took them in for you yesterday. I think they'll fit. And you may have my buckled shoes too."

"Oh, Kuza!" was all I could say. I ought to have thanked her properly, but I could only put my hand on her coverlet for a moment. Kuza had bought these town clothes with the money she earned. She did not dare to wear them in the house — Father forbade it — but occasionally when she went into town she took them with her secretly and changed on the way. How did she know that I was dreading the thought of taking the exam in my dark *katrinza* and homespun blouse, with clumsy *opanken* on my feet?

I went to Kuza's chest and opened it. On top lay the blouse and skirt, which were just the same as the ones the girls wore in the cities. I put them on and suddenly felt quite grown up. The flat black shoes fitted me perfectly, as if I had bought them for myself at Moishe's. I wished that Mr. Morianu and Marcel could see me. I pushed open one half of the casement window and tried to see my reflection against the glass. Out in the yard, Father was hitching Huza to the light farm cart.

Meanwhile, Kuza had been getting up too and before I left the room I hastily put an arm round her neck, as if I were doing something forbidden, and I gave her a kiss.

I hurried into the kitchen to wash myself. The fresh water cooled my eyes, but it could not wash away my nervousness. As I was drying my hands and face, Father and Mother came into the kitchen together. I was just going to explain about the clothes, but I did not get a chance.

"And what does this mean, pray?" roared Father, and he gripped the sleeve of the white blouse in his rough fingers. "Where do you think you're going, Miss? To a circus?"

His voice cracked. I retreated a step with my back to the stove. Mother looked at me.

"Don't shout so, Burda!" she said to Father, but he was too worked up to listen.

"You're not a city woman — you're my daughter, a peasant's daughter! Off with you now, and change those clothes. And don't let me see you like that again, ever!"

Father was in such a rage that he kicked out at a wooden settle near the stove and it fell over, grazing my leg. It hurt and I had to bite my lips together not to whimper. That would only have infuriated Father more.

"Go and change, Annuzza," said Mother, as she hustled me out of the kitchen. My leg was painful and it seemed a dreadful omen for the rest of the day. When I got back to my room, I could tell by Kuza's look that she had heard Father shouting and that she knew why. She did not say a word, but helped me to change. My clean linen blouse was much coarser and rougher than the one from the city. It felt as hard as a board round my shoulders. Wearing everyday clothes and *opanken*, it was hard to believe that I should ever get as far as the town that day. When I followed Kuza into the kitchen, neither Father nor Bunika was there. Mother made a sign to me to climb up onto the cart. Puiu was fixing a red aster behind Huzu's blinker.

"That's so he'll know it's important, taking someone to an exam," he called out to me.

That's nice of him, I thought, and climbed up to the driving seat. Mother held the reins loosely in her hands, for Huzu knew when to start, and we drove off. Kuza went with us as far as the gate. She held my hand and I could feel her fingers pressing mine. I knew what she was trying to say. The cart rumbled over the path between the fields toward the high road. Before it curved away, I looked back once more. In the morning light, the low slate roof hung like a dark blanket over the paleness of the house. The brown streak in the distance was Kuza's arm. She was waving to me and I knew that she would be thinking of me as we drove along the highway.

Although I had often been to the town with Mother before, it seemed an endless journey that day. The air was so clear that you imagined you were looking through a pane of highly polished glass. You could even see the peaks of the Carpathians to the west and southwest. Our direction was northeast, toward the big town on the Prut River. On previous occasions, I had always played a secret game on the way to market. I used to weave fairy tales into the landscape about a castle that only I could see, rising above the tall fir trees. The wind blew the castle from hill to hill and there lived a peasant's daughter who had been changed into a princess by a huge bear. I always looked hard to see if I could catch sight of a real bear. Drago thought that there were still some alive in in the Carpathian Mountains.

That day, however, I was too impatient to get to the town to build castles on the hills. I had never made the journey in late autumn before, for we usually went in the summer, with goods to sell, setting out before dawn in order to be there in good time. Nor had I seen much of the town, for Mother would make straight for the market place and I would sit by her side until everything was sold. If Mother had business elsewhere, I looked after Huzu and the cart. We always went back to the village the same way we had come.

As we came within sight of the plains by the Prut River, Mother stopped the cart. She bent down and groped under the seat for a parcel.

"Here," she said, handing it to me, "put them on."

This was the first time she had spoken since we left home, although that did not surprise me, for she never had much to say.

I took the packet and untied the string. There were the shoes — Kuza's black, low-cut shoes.

"Mamika, Mamika," I stammered. "You . . . you . . ."

"Don't talk so much." Mother jerked the reins and Huzu went on. Now at least I had decent shoes to wear. I should not feel quite so ashamed of myself as in my shabby *opanken*.

I had never felt so grateful to Mother in my life. For the first time it occurred to me that she would be pleased if I got through. It was a bit silly, I know, but suddenly I felt braver and more confident. As we drove into the suburbs, my hands were no longer glued together nervously as they had been when we set out. I could look round and I could concentrate. I did not think much of the brown and gray houses we were passing. They were not nearly as gay as those in our village, in my opinion. Until then, the town had always meant big stone buildings, paved streets, well-dressed people, glossy horses, and shiny cars. Now I saw that there was another town too, the one Drago had known, the town of the lonely and the poor. Perhaps living here wasn't so desirable after all!

The cart rolled past the station. Huzu puffed and pulled, for the slope uphill into the center of the town was quite steep. The Town Hall Square I knew already. In the middle was a big memorial surrounded by a patch of grass which was turning an autumnal brown. Trolley cars overtook us, jangling. Huzu pricked his ears and I had to smile, for he suddenly began to prance like the cab horses we passed in the streets. Up in the tower of the Town Hall, I could see the fire patrol pacing up and down.

We turned into a broad street that I had never seen before and I could not imagine how Mother knew the way. Had she asked beforehand, I wondered. I saw a big building that looked like a church, but there was no cross on the dome. When I asked her what it was, she said briefly, "That's the synagogue."

I had no idea what a synagogue was, but there was so much that I wanted to see that I had no time to ask her. What puzzled me most of all were the trees that lined the street. They were so strange, standing in rows like the laths of a fence, and they all looked identical. I could not account for this at all, for I knew perfectly well that no two trees are alike.

Mother must have noticed my astonishment, for she said, "The trees here are all lopped and

trimmed, Annuzza. They are not allowed to grow
naturally as they do in the countryside. It's the
same with the people. They don't always live as
they would like to either."

I was not sure what she meant — something to
do with the squalid, dingy houses in the suburbs,
perhaps. But again I did not question her further,
for we had come in sight of a long, sprawling red-
brick building, with colored windows that glistened like a string of beads in the sunlight. The
green dome in the center of the building looked so
light and airy, it might have been spinning in the
breeze.

"What's that?" I asked.

"That's where the Archbishop lives, and this is
where we stop."

When I thought about the drive later, I realized
that I had taken in everything except the people. I
simply hadn't noticed them at all.

We had come to a building that looked to me
like a gigantic white box with green windows and
a big green door. It was rather like a barn door, I
decided, as I jumped down from the cart.

Mother made no sign that she was getting down
with me. It had not occurred to me that I should
have to go in by myself.

"I expect it's time for you to go in," said Mother.
"When I've finished at the market, I'll come back
and wait for you here." That was all. She whipped
up the horse, and the cart disappeared.

I was alone.

Just as I was summoning up courage to walk up the steps to the front door, I saw a group of girls approaching. They were hardly taller than I, and yet they looked different and much older. I stood still and let them pass. They were all laughing and talking very fast, as if they had something important to say that could not wait. They wore plain black dresses with white collars and they made my peasant clothes look conspicuous, like a masquerade costume. Their hair was long and it floated loosely with every step. They wore navy berets like little saucers and there was a gold-embroidered badge in front. Not one of them so much as noticed I was there.

I followed them into the school, keeping my distance, but after the first few steps, I stood still. The floor was so highly polished that it shone like the ice on the village pond in winter. The vaulted ceiling was as high as the one in church at home. Taking care not to slip, for I was not used to shoes, I tiptoed a little farther. All I could see were high doors, all painted the identical green and all shut. The girls disappeared through one of them and I could not think of anything else to do but follow. My heart was thumping as it did when I was buying my beads. If anything, I was even more excited.

I turned the handle of the door through which the girls had vanished and entered the room timidly. There I got quite a shock. This room too was as big as a great hall, and there were rows and rows of benches, painted the inevitable green, and they were full of girls with serious expressions, all wearing black dresses and white collars. I felt that you could not distinguish one from the other, any more than the trees in the streets. As if there had been some inaudible command, they all turned their heads and stared at me.

"Are you looking for someone?" a voice asked.

Only then did I see a teacher's desk and the lady who sat behind it. She was young with fair hair and had friendly eyes like Kuza's.

"I've come to take the entrance examination," I whispered.

"That's in another classroom," she said. "Show her the way, Zaruk."

One of the girls in the front row stood up immediately and walked toward me.

"This way," she told me.

I followed the girl through a long corridor, up a wide staircase and along another corridor. She did not speak to me. I don't belong here, I thought, that's why she doesn't say anything. It dawned on me suddenly that perhaps I shouldn't like this school after all, any more than I liked the mean little houses in the suburbs, and the trees that had to be held in check as if they were dangerous dogs. In our village, they could grow as they pleased.

The girl stopped abruptly and I nearly bumped into her, I was so preoccupied. "This is it," she said, and went on, leaving me alone.

Another green door, I thought. By the time I opened it, ill at ease and confused, I was not at all sure that I wanted to pass.

The children in this classroom were not dressed in black, and there were even some peasant children with hair rigidly parted in the center like mine. There was no teacher's platform, but a long table stood in front of the blackboard at which were seated several men and women. They did not seem to have anything to do and were fidgeting with penholders or turning the leaves of exercise books.

"Come over here," said one of the men, who reminded me of the stranger in the sleigh, although it was not he. He asked me my name and where I came from and told me that I was late. He spoke softly but it was a reprimand all the same and I apologized. Then I was told to sit down at one of the green benches with the other girls, and the examination I had longed for and feared for so many months had begun.

Afterwards, when it was all over and I was driving home by Mother's side, I came to the conclusion that examinations aren't an ordeal once you stop being afraid. I wrote the essay, tackled the arithmetic, and then answered the oral questions. By the time I was asked to say a poem, all my anxiety had gone. I stood in front of the blackboard and started:

> *Beyond the yellow fields*
> *And the lush woods . . .*

As I recited, there was silence in the examination hall. The teachers looked at me and I saw them nod to one another. Why, I did not know. A great many of the things that happened to me that morning passed me by, shadowy and unreal. Often I had the feeling that it was all a dream, particularly the hours we had to wait afterwards under the supervision of one of the teachers while our papers were being marked and the results prepared.

How different it was in our village where everybody knew everyone else. Here we were all strangers. Now and then, someone would whisper to her neighbor. Then there was silence again. Next to me was a girl in a red dress. Her brown hair hung loose to her shoulders and she took no notice of me. No one there knew that my name was Annuzza, that we owned the loveliest maize field in the village, and that I had been to the harvest dance, the *klaka*. Probably I should never see the girl again. I can't possibly have passed, I thought.

At last a door opened and all the examiners filed into the classroom with solemn faces. They were led by an elderly white-haired gentleman whom I had not seen in the examination room.

He had a sheet of paper in his hand, and he stood in front of the rows of forms and made a speech. He spoke like Father Stanescu, slowly and with dignity. His words sailed past me like clouds in a summer sky. Surely he must be going to read the names of the successful candidates soon.

Then I heard him say, "And now I am going to read the pass list . . ."

Wasn't it all the same to me if I passed or not? No, no. I had been deceiving myself. It did matter, it mattered a lot. I pressed my palms together as I always did when I got excited.

The old man's voice seemed to come from far away.

"Alasch, Avardescu, Balan, Bedeanu, Bilu." And now? Who came next?

"Burda," he said, as if it were obvious.

I felt the blood leave my cheeks. The other girls mentioned had all stood up and sat down again and I did the same, although standing had somehow become a most difficult thing to do, my knees were wobbling so.

I had passed! I had passed!

As I sat beside Mother going home, her face showed no emotion. All the same, I thought that she was pleased, for she said several times, "There's bread and bacon just by you. Go on, eat! You must be hungry."

She had never said that to me on the way home before.

In the linen satchel that I held on my knees there were papers with instructions for the beginning of term, school rules about behavior, and conditions of maintenance in the boarding annex. My hand stroked them from time to time and the paper crackled. It was all right. I had got through.

What would they say in the village, Father and Kuza and Bunika, the teacher, and the other children?

It did not feel a bit like a homecoming that day, for in a week or so I should be leaving the village again, this time for good, so I thought.

Chapter 11

BREAKING THE NEWS

A FEW HOURS LATER we were home. As Mother
and I walked into the kitchen, Bunika, Father,
Kuza, and Puiu were sitting round the table. I felt
as though a storm were brewing, threatening to
break as soon as the first word was uttered.

Mother, on the contrary, behaved as if nothing in
particular had happened. She went to the stove
and made up the fire and she said quite casually,
"She'll be leaving for the city, Annuzza will."

Kuza jumped up and came over to me as if to
be ready to protect me from something. I looked
at Father uneasily. He was standing now. I could
tell that he had been drinking and I knew that he
was often unpredictable in his rage, but he just
stood there, not saying a word, although his silence

seemed to cost him an effort, for he leaned heavily on the table for support.

He looked at me as if we were strangers. Then he muttered an oath and spat on the ground close to my feet. His hand reached out for a cudgel that was standing against the wall, and I winced instinctively, afraid that he was going to beat me. But he turned away and stumped heavily out of the kitchen. Out in the yard, I could hear him shouting at the farmhands. Then there was silence.

Bunika's fingers were twitching, Puiu just grinned and said, "I'll take over the hens from you now. I bet the buzzard'll be sorry."

"Shut up!" cried Kuza.

"Poor thing, poor little thing," mumbled Bunika.

I put my head on Kuza's shoulder and felt my eyes filling with tears. I did so long for someone to say to me, "Well done, Annuzza!" or "I'm sure it can't have been easy for you." It was quite likely that both Mother and Kuza were pleased about it, but they did not actually say so. Bunika, on the contrary, was really sorry for me. Puiu was glad because it meant that he could take over my chores on the farm, and Father was angry.

I began to think that I was indeed a "poor little thing," more to be pitied than congratulated. I remembered how Drago had expressed it up in the mountains: "All at once, you find that you don't belong to the village any more nor to the city either." Was he right?

As the kitchen door opened I raised my head, but it was not Father as I had thought; it was Puiu going out.

"Lay the table, Annuzza. It's time for supper," said Mother. "Then you'd better see to the hens."

It was good to get out of doors into the evening air. The yellow moon hung like a ripe pumpkin in the sky. If the mountain pastures had not been so far away, I should have run to see Drago. He would understand.

Inside the hen-house, I bent down and Mikuza the Second pushed her way to the front. I took her in my arms and held her a little. How warm hens are! Ours weren't a bit afraid of me. Now they would have to get used to Puiu.

Suddenly I heard the clatter of a wagon coming along the path from the village. I locked the hen-house and ran round to the veranda. I could not see much in the dark, but when the cart turned into the gateway, I could make out two figures on the driving seat, and as it stopped, I recognized the teacher and Moishe.

"There she is!" I heard Puiu shout and realized that he was there as well, sitting behind the others in the cart.

Mr. Morianu came straight across to me.

"Congratulations, Annuzza," he said, giving me his hand. "I'm very glad for your sake, and I feel a bit pleased with myself, too."

The teacher had never shaken hands with me

before. I was so bewildered that I could not say a word, but it did not matter, for Moishe was already talking his head off.

"It's a bargain, I tell you, a real bargain! The young lady's going to the city, isn't she? She'll need a school uniform, won't she? I've brought some cloth with me and I tell you, Miss, I swear to you, I've had nothing to touch it for quality these twenty years . . ." and he went rattling on.

Meanwhile, Mother had opened the door and asked both men in.

I stayed in the yard and sat down on the faded grass, but I could still hear Moishe's voice from the kitchen, and it grated on my nerves. So I got up again and wandered slowly out through the gate, drawn toward the maize field as if the familiar cornstalks could answer all my questions.

"Annuzza!"

Marcel's unmistakable voice made me turn and I saw him running swift and light-footed as a hare.

"Marcel," I said softly as he pulled up near me.

"Puiu's just told me. I met him in the village."

"Did you?" was all I could say.

"But you'll come back, won't you?"

I shrugged my shoulders.

"You will," he said and, with an embarrassed gesture, he took something from his belt and thrust it in my hands.

"Here you are," he said. "So that you can play a *doina* sometimes in the city."

Before I could say thank you, Marcel had dashed off again.

It was a reed pipe, Marcel's own. I held it in both hands. This day has been so full, I thought, crammed full like Kuza's clothes chest. You just couldn't get any more into one single day. . . .

A little later I sat in the field. The pipe was cool and fresh to my lips. Like everyone else in the village, I can play a little and I tried a *doina*. The tune sounded sad, like a farewell to all I had known of life so far.

Chapter 12

GOOD-BYE TO THE VILLAGE

MOTHER BOUGHT the black material from Moishe and made my school dress and Kuza embroidered the white collar for it. Puiu took over the hens next morning and Father did not expect me to do any more work at home. As soon as I started looking round for something useful to do Mother would say, "Leave that, Annuzza. You'd better be getting your things straight," or she would send me to one of our neighbors to say good-bye.

So passed one long week of my life in which I belonged neither to the village nor the town. I felt as if I were floating in midstream with the current carrying me along, but I could not reach either bank.

Wherever I went, people wished me luck and everyone brought me presents to take with me into the town. They were just trifles, but they filled my chest to the brim. Our neighbor on the right brought me a *colak*, a sweetish braided white bread, so that I should not starve in the town as she feared. Father Stanescu gave me a little shrine with folding doors and said, "May your path be blessed, my child." Mr. Morianu gave me lots of good advice and a fountain pen. I had never owned one before, and I was very proud of it.

It was on one of these last days that I made my way up the mountain to say good-bye to Drago. I had only a few hours with him, for I had to be back in the village by evening.

As I told him the news, sitting next to him on the bench outside his hut, he did not seem to be surprised. He just nodded and said: "I knew it, I knew it, Annuzza."

I told him all about the examination and although he did not comment at all, I knew he had been listening attentively and that was a lot. It was almost as if I had confided my thoughts to a sheet of paper. In the hours that followed, I placed many of my worries in Drago's hands.

Just as I was leaving, Drago pulled out a silver coin from the pocket in his belt. "Here is a *taler*, Annuzza. You can't buy anything with it these days, but it may bring you luck. It's a good thing to have a *taler* in the town. And when you're there, don't forget Mikuza and the buzzard. The town can tear your heart out too, if you're not careful. Keep your eyes open all the way, so that you'll be able to find the road back again, if you want to."

My heart swelled, and Drago's words sounded in my ears as I turned and left. He stood in front of his hut and took out his flute, and his shepherd's song accompanied me as I walked, soaring like the song of a bird high over the beech trees. Then it grew softer and fainter until I could hear it no longer.

On the day I was leaving, I changed into a city girl for the first time. I put away my peasant clothes and slipped into my school uniform. The white collar was as becoming as a necklace. From now on I should wear black and white every day like all the other girls at school. This is what it said in the School Regulations, which I had read so often that I knew them by heart:

"During official hours, the pupils of the Lyceul Orthodox must wear only the approved uniform, whether at school, at home, or in the street. The uniform consists of a plain straight black frock, a white linen collar (instructions for *broderie anglaise* pattern at the end of the brochure), a blue beret, gray lisle stockings, and black shoes. The school badge is a blue triangle on which the initials 'L.O.' are embroidered in gold thread with the pupil's school number clearly marked below it.

This badge must be worn on the sleeve, so that the school and the pupil attending it can be readily identified. A similar blue felt badge with the school's initials is to be stitched on the school beret. Pupils may wear only plain navy-blue coats, with the addition of a gray fur collar in winter if they wish. The pupil's school number must also be sewn on the right coat sleeve. All high school pupils are expected to conduct themselves impeccably in the street. If anyone should misbehave, her number will enable her to be reported to the authorities forthwith."

The horse and cart were waiting for me, just as they had been on the day of the examination. Father and Puiu had stacked my clothes chest at the back and Mother was to drive me into town. I was wearing Kuza's low black shoes, which she had given me as a present.

For the last time until the holidays, I went into the kitchen where Bunika was sitting in her usual seat. She kept clearing her throat as if there were something in the air that irritated her and she mumbled as softly as ever, "Here's a bag of sweets for you. Mind you don't break your teeth on them."

"Good-bye, Bunika," I said.

Puiu stood on the veranda and presented me with a dried corncob. "The hens'll be all right," he assured me, grinning as ever.

Father stroked Huzu with his rough fingers and all he said was, "Well, there."

But Kuza scrambled on to the cart beside me and rode with me to the end of the village. "But you'll be back for the holidays and for my wedding!" she said, and tried to laugh.

Then she jumped down and disappeared into the cloud of dust the wheels threw up. She was lost from sight, like the village, the fields, and all that had been my world until that day.

I held the shining corncob tightly in my hand all the way. Mother suddenly turned to me and placed a little leather purse on my knee.

"If you get too homesick, here's your fare home. I had some money over from the tablecloths you worked in the winter."

I loosened the cord round the purse and my fingers shook. There was money inside. It clinked and rattled and shone. Dear Mother! Only Huzu could not speak, but he was as shrewd as all his breed and kept pricking his ears and turning his head toward me as if he wanted me to know that he would not forget me either.

Would the people forget me, though, just as they had forgotten Drago in his time and would I find a home for myself in the city?

Even if I went away, the village, the maize field, the farm, everything remained. This thought comforted me. It was like a tree against which I could lean.

I never knew till then that you could feel so happy and so sad at the same time.

Chapter 13

HIGH SCHOOL PUPIL

F OR SEVERAL WEEKS NOW, I had been nothing more than a number, simply six hundred and ninety-nine among seven hundred and fifty others. 699 was the number I wore on a blue triangle on the sleeve of my black school dress. If someone had to give me a name it was always "Burda." I gradually forgot that I had a Christian name.

In class I sat next to a girl who hardly ever spoke to me. She would only whisper occasionally to ask me an answer she did not know. Her name was Mafalda Anelimonte and her father was the Italian Consul. I was sure she considered that socially she was much my superior.

At recess, Mafalda was always up to something. For instance, it was she who suggested, "Let's stick

pins in the teacher's cushion," or "Shall we put a
damp cloth on her chair?" The other girls thought
that Mafalda was marvelous, but I could not make
friends with her. It was all too strange and new.

My school work presented no difficulties and I
usually worked out my homework in my head as
I walked back to the boarding annex from school.
At first, I used to tuck myself away in a remote
corner of the big hall with my books. It was only
gradually that I realized that no one here was
going to forbid me to study or read. This was so
novel to me that I could hardly grasp it for a while,
but eventually I came to take it for granted.

I slept in a dormitory with five other girls. My
bed was soft and warm, but in spite of the comfort
I often felt cold, I was so lonely. There was no one
to call out a friendly "Good morning, Annuzza!"
on my way to school. Nowhere was there a face
I knew. People either looked away or straight
through me, as if I were made of glass. Everyone
walked fast, as if they were always in a hurry.

The school itself and the annex both seemed to
me much noisier than our kitchen at home or the
fields near the farm. I was always surrounded by
loud voices speaking very quickly. Even when I
lay in bed after lights out, the other girls went on
chattering to each other. They talked about the
teachers, they told each other about their homes,
they discussed films. I had never even been to a
movie. Anything I might have told them about the

village would obviously have bored them, so I preferred to hold my tongue. Often when I was alone,
I brought out Marcel's flute and played a *doina*.

The five girls were all daughters of big landowners who lived on their estates outside the town.
They all went home at midday on Saturday and
came back in time for lessons on Monday morning.
During the weekends, I used to play a game with
myself. I pretended that I was one of them, and I
joined in their conversations. I let them call me
Annuzza and in my make-believe my father was a
landed proprietor like theirs.

I sat on my bed and I talked as fast as the others.
"And do you know," I told them, as they
gathered round me, "our estate is huge, more than
twelve hundred acres. We have an enormous house
with dozens of rooms. Mine is decorated in green
and white. We own forty horses and there are lots
of cows and I couldn't even count the hens. When
you see our sheep in a flock, their backs look like
a vast lake. There is a park in front of the house
and the trees are all tall and straight and neatly
trimmed. My grandmother has a big pitcher and
it's full of golden coins. We often give parties for
the neighbors. Father hires musicians and there are
lanterns in the trees and we all dance."

I could go on like this for hours. It was sheer
invention, of course, but there were times when
I really forgot that I was a peasant girl.

One Sunday I asked the house mistress if I

could go for a walk and she said I could. I put
on the new blue coat that Mother had sent me not
long before, and I arranged my beret in front of
the mirror. I was satisfied that I looked as if I had
been a city child all my life.

As I reached the street, it started snowing. The
flakes clung to my shoulders and my hair. Thicker
and faster they fell, noiselessly gliding over the
roofs and the pavements of the town. I walked and
walked. Gradually the scene before me changed
and I thought I must be dreaming, and shaking
the blue glass ball on the shelf at home. It was
winter in the town, and now I was actually living
through it. As it grew dark, the street lamps came
on and the people in their houses switched on
bright electric lights, turning night into day.

Nearly every day I saw something else that was
new and strange, but I was getting to know the
school building and where all the corridors led.

In the annex, the girls changed their uniforms
for ordinary clothes in the afternoons, so I decided to buy myself a blue skirt and white blouse
with the money Mother had given me. I had not
worn my *katrinza* and homespun blouse since I
came. I was Burda now, a first-year pupil at the
highly respectable Lyceul Orthodox, and no longer
Annuzza, the barefoot peasant child.

So the days and weeks passed. Then something
happened that gave my school life a sudden twist.

Chapter 14

NADINE

IT WAS MONDAY MORNING. The teacher had left
the classroom after the second period and as
usual I sat alone at my desk. The others had
gathered into little groups and were all busy
talking.

Then a girl whose surname was Jeschan, and
who had joined our class only the week before,
came up to me. She was smaller than I, and she
sat three rows behind me. I thought she was pretty,
with dainty, delicate features, like a big doll.

"What's your first name, Burda?" she asked me.

"Annuzza," I answered, and just to say my name
again seemed to cheer me up.

"Mine's Nadine," she declared, and smiled at me.

"I've never heard of it," I said.

"It's a Polish name. My grandmother came from Warsaw, you know, and she settled here a long time ago."

I nodded.

"She was a famous dancer, the *prima ballerina* at the Warsaw Opera. When the company came on tour here, she met my grandfather and married him and stayed. I've been learning dancing this past year. Can you dance, Annuzza?"

"Oh, yes," I said, "I can do the *hora* and the *moldovenesca* and the *sarba* too," mentioning our favorite peasant dances.

"What about ballet?" asked Nadine.

I shook my head. I did not even know what ballet was, and I was just going to ask her when the bell rang and Nadine jumped up and went back to her desk.

All through the next lesson, I kept thinking about this strange conversation and wondering whether Nadine would come and speak to me again, or if I could summon up the courage to go over to her desk.

At recess after the next lesson, we had to leave our classrooms. Until that day, I had always spent the time alone in a corner near the window. No one had taken any notice of me. It was wonderful when Nadine came straight up to me, slipped her arm through mine, and we went out into the corridor together. I wanted to squeeze her arm tight in sheer gratitude, but I did not dare.

"You know, Annuzza, Mother's been saying for weeks that I think far too much about dancing and that I ought to make friends with another girl and invite her home. She says we need friends at our age, but I started the term late and all the girls in our class have made friends already. You're the only one who's always alone, so I wondered if you'd like to be my friend, Annuzza, and come to our house sometimes."

My heart jumped with excitement. Nadine actually wanted us to be friends! I had never had a friend before.

I wanted to shout aloud, "Yes, I will!" for everyone to hear, but instead, I just nodded hard.

"Good," said Nadine. "Come round this afternoon. Where do you live, by the way?"

"I'm a boarder at the annex," I said.

"I'll come for you about four then. I think that'll be best," said Nadine.

I could hardly wait for the afternoon. I was as excited as I had been about buying my beads and about the maize *klaka*. I could already see myself dressed in my new blue skirt and white blouse and my school coat. I wondered if I should take my flute to show Nadine that even if I could not dance a ballet, whatever that was, I could at least play a *doina*.

By three o'clock, I had done my homework. I changed my clothes, brushed my hair, and pinned up my braid tidily. Then I went to the window and waited for Nadine. I kept looking at the clock on the wall. As the big finger moved past the twelve for four o'clock, I felt empty with disappointment, I was so sure that Nadine had changed her mind and decided not to come.

A few minutes later, I saw her coming round the corner. I pushed open the casement window and called out: "Wait there, I'm coming down!" I snatched up my coat and beret in great haste, and put them on as I tore down the stairs. The afternoon with Nadine was the only thing I could think of. At the bottom of the staircase, two of the girls from my dormitory were standing talking.

"I'm going to see my friend!" I shouted to them, although they had not asked me where I was going. But I had to tell someone that I had a friend of my own.

I reached the street in a few seconds and there was Nadine to meet me, laughing. It was only then that I noticed that her hair had a reddish gleam under her blue school beret and that her eyes were shining and blue.

"Hello, Annuzza!" she said and took my arm at once. It seemed like a dream. She had said "Hello, Annuzza," as if we were at home in the village. But this was even better.

I hardly spoke as we walked to her parents' house, but Nadine did not stop talking. She spoke very fast, like a fountain bubbling. She told me about her parents and her ballet classes and the summer holidays she had spent in Dorna Vatra.

"I must tell you, Annuzza," she said. "At the hotel there was a children's party and I danced a solo in a pink dress with ballet shoes to match. Everyone clapped like mad when I'd finished. I want to be a *prima ballerina* like my grandmother when I'm grown up. I want to dance at the Bucharest Opera and perhaps in Vienna, too."

When we pulled up a little later in front of a wrought-iron gate and Nadine paused for a moment, I felt as if I had known the girl at my side for a long time. And yet her world was as new to me as everything else in the town.

"This is where I live," said Nadine, and pressed a button. There was a humming noise from somewhere and the gate opened automatically. We went in and up a gravel path as broad as the high road through our village, toward a big yellow house. It's practically a castle, I thought, but later on I discovered that you called them villas and that there were many others scattered through the town. Still, my first impression was so overwhelming that I have never forgotten it.

I kept stopping to stare until Nadine took my hand and pulled me toward the door. "Oh, do come on!" she exclaimed impatiently.

As we went up the steps, a young girl in a black frock came to meet us. She reminded me a little of Kuza. I was just wondering if I ought to curtsy to her as I had seen the other girls do at school, when Nadine whispered, "That's the maid."

We went through the front door into the hall and Nadine threw her coat carelessly over a chair. I could not take my eyes off the room. The walls were covered with pictures in gilt frames and you could not see the floor for carpets.

"That's my father," said Nadine.

I looked around but could see no one.

"On the wall — there!" Nadine said, laughing, and pointing to one of the portraits. I wondered if the movies the other girls raved about in school were something like this. Everything seemed so unreal — the house, the hall with its dark, elaborate furniture, the carpets, Nadine herself.

"Isn't your hall as big?" asked Nadine.

I shook my head.

"I think smaller ones are much cosier," declared Nadine, trying to put me at my ease.

I ought to have told her there and then that our hall, if you could call it a hall, was just a narrow passage, that I was a peasant, and that I had never been inside a house like this in my life. But my lips were pressed hard together, as if they were determined not to let a single word slip past. I was afraid that Nadine would have nothing to do with me if I told her the truth. Even as it was, I was surprised that she had invited me to her home. Nadine could have had any girl in the class for her friend.

In the midst of my thoughts I heard Nadine say,

as if she owed me an explanation, "My father collects pictures. What does yours collect?"

I shrugged my shoulders. How could I confess that my father didn't collect anything except, perhaps, empty schnapps bottles?

Nadine seemed not to notice my silence. Light as a feather, she darted through the house ahead of me. She told me that her father was a doctor and that her mother traveled about a good deal.

"Mummy's always off to some spa or other, or paying a visit to Vienna, and I'm left by myself. Even when she is at home, we usually have guests. Until this year I've always had a governess, so I've never had school friends like other girls. Have you ever had a real friend?"

I shook my head.

"That's fine," said Nadine. "Mother's been at home a lot more recently and she thinks I must be lonely. But it will be all right now that you're my friend, won't it?"

I nodded. Could you say, "Now that you're my friend," just like that? I would never have dared, but if Nadine said it, it must be right.

"Why are you walking on tiptoe?" Nadine asked me suddenly. She could not possibly have guessed that we always walked on tiptoe over a carpet in order to save it.

"Oh, I just felt like it," I replied, and tried to tread more heavily on the thick pile.

Then Nadine led me up a curved staircase to

her room. But it wasn't a room at all, I gasped to myself. It was an ornamental flower garden, a meadow in bloom. I stood at the door, not daring to go in.

There was a pale green carpet on the floor. The chairs were curved like shells and covered with a tapestry that seemed to blossom with all the spring flowers I had ever seen. There was a sofa to match and the afternoon sun streamed through the curtains setting off the gay colors. Along one wall ran a glass shelf on which sat a delightful collection of stuffed animals.

"That's my zoo," said Nadine and she flicked a little brown monkey so that it somersaulted on to the floor. "Do sit down, Annuzza. Would you like to see me dance?"

I nodded.

Nadine went to a light oak box and lifted up the lid. Music started to play and Nadine stood on tiptoe and began to dance, floating through the room like a snowflake. How beautifully she dances, I thought. It was very different from our peasant dances.

The door opened and suddenly a young lady came in. Nadine ran to meet her, flung her arms round her neck, and gave her a kiss. Then she led her to where I was sitting.

"This is my friend Annuzza, Mummy," she said.

So that was Nadine's mother! But how could you do a thing like that, throw your arms round your mother's neck and kiss her? Nadine talked to her as if she were a girl like us.

Mrs. Jeschan said, "Good afternoon, Annuzza," and gave me her hand. I took it nervously. It was as small and soft as a child's, and I was afraid I might hurt it. I managed to bob a curtsy.

"You're from the country, aren't you?" she asked.

"Yes," I said softly, feeling shy.

"I expect your parents have an estate there?"

I nodded. Our farm was a big one for a peasant's. Perhaps it counted as a small estate, I stilled my conscience.

"Do come and see Nadine very often. She's so much alone," said Mrs. Jeschan. "And have a nice time, both of you."

Then she went away again with a friendly nod in my direction.

From that day on, I led a double life. At one stroke I had invented a make-believe Annuzza, false to my village, my parents, and the maize field too. I had bought Nadine's friendship with a lie.

All the same, things went very well.

I spent nearly every other afternoon with Nadine. Gradually I got used to her beautiful surroundings. I romanced endlessly about our "estate," inventing new tales about the life there and the way we entertained.

I avoided saying anything directly about my parents or myself and soothed my conscience by telling myself that I was only sharing my secret dreams with Nadine.

The girls in the annex were not slow to discover that I had found a friend. I do not know if that was why they became more sociable, but sometimes they even called me Annuzza and when we lay in bed in the evenings, they no longer ignored me as they used to.

It was only at school that I was still "Burda." I was one of the best students in the class, and the others often asked me to help them, but except for Nadine, no one called me Annuzza.

So the first few months passed and I went home for the Christmas holidays. I saw everything with different eyes. The house seemed to have shrunk, and for the first time in my life I noticed how rough and work-coarsened were Mother's hands. It occurred to me, too, that Father was only sober in the mornings. Only Kuza seemed as beautiful as ever.

When I went back to school in January, I left my *katrinza* and peasant blouse at home. I did not need them any more. Now less than ever did I know where I belonged. The village was still the focus of my life as it used to be, but in the city lived Nadine, and she was my best friend.

Chapter 15

TRUTH AND FALSEHOOD

F OR SEVERAL WEEKS NOW I had sat next to Nadine
in class. We had asked to be allowed to sit
together. At recess we went about arm-in-arm,
along the corridors or around the playground. Even
during lessons we kept whispering. We always
had something to tell each other that couldn't
wait. I knew all about Nadine's life, and she
thought she knew all about mine.

For other children, having a friend was something they seemed able to take for granted. But
to me it was a fresh source of wonder every day.
Only at night in bed did the tales I had invented
for Nadine's benefit crowd round me menacingly.
Sometimes I felt as if I were alone in a forest
during a storm. The lightning struck the surround-

ing trees and they fell on top of me, Annuzza, the landowner's daughter, burying me beneath them. It was like a nightmare. I shivered under the thick blankets as if I were lying in the snow. Each time I made up my mind that I would tell Nadine the truth the very next day, but when morning came, it all looked different, and I was more worried about losing her friendship than about being found out.

Mother seldom came to market during the winter. We had an understanding with our neighbor Munteanu, and if we had any produce for sale then, he would take it into town on his sleigh. In return, Mother would carry his eggs and butter and cheese to market in the summer. We had the better cart and he had a more reliable sleigh.

When I lived in the village, I resented this arrangement, which had existed as long as I could remember. I longed to drive into the town with Mother through the countryside when it was covered with snow. Now I was glad of it, for there seemed no danger that Mother would come and visit me at school. If Nadine saw Mother in her peasant clothes, I should be caught fast in the network of my romancing like a fly in a spider's web.

Then one day it happened.

The Latin lesson was almost over when there was a knock on the door and in walked Muschu, the janitor.

"Will Burda please go to the principal's office?"

"Do you know what it's for?" asked Nadine.

I shook my head.

I left the classroom and waited outside the principal's door. Suppose he had found out that I had been telling lies? A pupil at the highly respectable Lyceul Orthodox did not tell lies, and perhaps I should be sent away, expelled, in accordance with the regulations.

I wiped my palms on the skirt of my dress and knocked.

"Come in," I heard the principal call.

I went in and curtsied.

The principal sat behind his desk which was as big as our kitchen range. I thought he must have heard the anxious beating of my heart, as I racked my brain for some excuse he might accept. But he simply said in a friendly voice: "Your mother's in the conference room next door. She'd like to have a word with you before she goes back."

So Mother had come to see me. I ought to have been delighted, for I had not seen her since Christmas. But there was no feeling of joy as I went through into the next room and stood there awkwardly before her. Why couldn't I run up to her and give her a hug, as Nadine would have done in my place?

"Good morning, Mother," I said stiffly.

"Annuzza!" said Mother. "How are you, child? You do look pale."

If only Nadine would not be waiting for me at the door! But she was sure to be hanging about, to find out why the principal had called me. I wished that Mother would at least wear city clothes when she came to market, but how could she? She didn't possess any, as I knew perfectly well. She was wearing a richly embroidered *katrinza* and a new headscarf. Everyone could see that she was a peasant. I wondered if there was any other door out of the room, and I searched around for a way of escape.

"What is the matter with you, Annuzza?" asked Mother.

"Nothing, nothing. I'm all right. I've done pretty well this term, honors for Latin and arithmetic and French. I might be one of the top ones this year, you know. I sit next to my friend Nadine now. We're having a sports gala soon and I'm playing in the school basketball team . . . It's . . ."

"Slowly, Annuzza, slowly! Goodness, how you gabble. . . ."

"I have to get back to my class now," I said.

Mother took a parcel out of the linen bag she had with her. "I've brought you some bacon from the last pig we killed and there are some eggs too. They're from Mikuza the Second."

Where on earth could I hide the stuff?

"I get plenty to eat, Mother."

"It's poor food you get in the towns," said Mother, thrusting the package into my hands.

Then she reached for the basket that she had set down on the floor.

"Huzu's waiting outside. I daresay he'd be pleased to see you," she said and turned to go.

I could hear voices and footsteps in the corridor.

"Won't you stay a bit, Mamika?" I asked hastily and held her by the sleeve.

"No, I can't, Annuzza. It's a long drive."

"Give them all my love at home," I said, as we left the conference room. The principal's office was empty, but the corridor was alive with girls. All the school's seven hundred and fifty pupils seemed to have packed into that one corridor at that very moment and they were all staring at us. I lowered my eyes, painfully embarrassed.

"Annuzza! Annuzza!"

It was Nadine. I saw her coming toward me.

"Wait here for me!" I called out. "I'll be back in a minute," and I hustled Mother to the entrance.

Was it really so or did I just imagine that Mother's eyes looked sad?

The farm cart was standing in front of the gate and Huzu whinnied as I ran up to him and patted his coat. I put my head on his neck.

"Give my love to the maize field, Huzu!" I whispered. He pricked up his ears. I couldn't think of anything else to say.

Mother climbed up onto the cart and took the reins in her hand.

"Don't forget that the trees in the town are all

stunted and lopped, Annuzza," she said, as she took her seat and drove off.

I nodded.

The cart continued on its way and I stood at the curb and waved, but Mother did not turn.

"Give Kuza my love, and the others too!" I called after her.

Then I was alone in the street, with the school towering behind me, and in front of me the empty square where the horse and cart had stood.

Slowly I turned and went back. Next time Mother comes, it'll be different, I promised myself. By then I should have told Nadine who I really was and where I came from.

Nadine dashed across the corridor toward me.

"Who was that, Annuzza?" she asked.

"Someone from the village," I answered reluctantly.

"One of the maids from home?" she asked.

"No. She's a peasant woman who lives in the village," I replied. "Come on, I must get through a couple of pages before next lesson."

I took Nadine by the hand and we ran up the stairs to our classroom. Now was the time to tell her, "That was my mother, Nadine. We're peasants, you know."

But I said nothing, although I felt thoroughly ashamed of myself. I knew that I was letting Mother down, and letting Nadine down, but most of all, I was letting myself down.

Chapter 16

NADINE'S COUSIN

TIME SLIPPED BY soft-footed. When I looked back on the three years I had been at the high school, they seemed incredibly short to me. It hardly seemed possible that I had celebrated my fifteenth birthday two months before at Nadine's.

I still loved dreaming to myself and when I had finished my homework I used to write little poems or stories which I kept in my satchel. It was my secret; not even Nadine knew about it, although we saw each other very often and were close friends.

I often asked myself what I was going to be, but I found no answer. There was a little mountain pass not far from our village, where there was

an echo. "What are you going to be, Annuzza?"
I called and the same words echoed back.

For the past year, I had been asked to tutor
two of the girls in the freshman class in grammar
and mathematics, and with the money I earned
I was able not only to take little presents home
when I went back for the holidays, but also to buy
myself a few clothes. I now had two dresses hanging in my closet — a red one with a white silk collar and a green one. When I went to Nadine's in
the afternoons I wore my school coat, and one of
the new dresses.

All the same, I still did not feel that I really belonged to the city, but neither was I a village child
any longer. I simply did not know where I stood.
I often thought of Drago and his shrewd words. I
had not forgotten the way back to the village, but
it was no longer my path in life. I was always glad
when the holidays came, but I had to recognize by
innumerable little signs that I was gradually becoming a stranger in my own home. Every time I
returned, things seemed to have shrunk: the
church seemed poky, my bed was too short, when
I went barefoot my feet hurt. Only the maize field
never altered. There I felt happiest; there I could
read and write and dream.

Many a time I had wanted to tell Nadine that
I was a peasant's daughter, but I had never done
so yet. I knew that I was a coward, but perhaps
that in itself made it more difficult for me to tell

her the truth. Without Nadine and her friendship, the city would have been a cold and empty place.

Mother had often come to see me at school since that first visit three years ago, but Nadine had never asked me about her again. Once, when she wanted to know why my parents never came to visit me, I told her that they sometimes came to the annex, and in any case I always spent my holidays at home with them. I was glad that Nadine seldom bothered me with questions.

Apart from seeing me several times a week, Nadine spent all her spare time dancing. She had joined the ballet school of the local branch of the National Theatre a year before and occasionally I was allowed in at rehearsals. I sat there enchanted in the front row. It was like living in a fairy tale. All around me were gilded railings, velvet hangings, the sparkle of crystal. Here it was that my dreams very nearly came true. This was the place for make-believe, for acting a part. Real life must wait outside. Here on the stage you could be anyone you wanted. Nadine was a famous dancer, almost a *prima ballerina,* and I was the landowner's daughter, Annuzza. My friendship with Nadine seemed to be the stage on which I performed my role. All the same, I could not help worrying about what would happen one day when the curtain fell.

I could tell by my clothes that I had grown. I had had my braid cut off a few months before and wore my hair short like a page-boy's. When Nadine's mother saw it for the first time she said, "It suits you, Annuzza. You look quite distinguished, full of personality."

I was not quite sure what she meant. How does personality look? As for "distinguished," I would have preferred by far to be beautiful, like Kuza, or even pretty like Nadine.

I had often met Marcel when I was home, either in the village street or out in the fields. He always went very red and I could feel my heart pounding a little. But he kept asking me the same question, "When are you coming back?" and I usually answered, "'Never." Sometimes I just shrugged my shoulders. Nevertheless, it was nice to know that he still wanted me to come back.

Whenever I played basketball at school I thought that I was rather like the ball flying through the air. I never knew whether I should just fall, or if someone would catch me, or if I would land in the basket.

Then came the day when I met Nelo for the first time. It was like a gala performance at the theatre for me, the first night of a new play in which I was starring.

Peasants are very superstitious, possibly because their lives can be made or marred by unexpected windfalls or little accidents. The yield from one harvest determines the whole standard of living for the coming year, but peasants' houses, stables, and barns are all made of wood and a single spark can ruin a man in a night. Being so vulnerable we are inclined to read our fate in trivial things, and we weigh the pros and cons of every good and bad sign.

My superstitions were as much a part of my luggage when I came to the city as the little shrine from the priest, or Mother's purse. True, I did not keep them in my clothes chest, but I carried them about with me and I clung to them tenaciously, although Nadine often laughed at me if she saw me clutch a button whenever I saw a chimney sweep, or make a wide curve to avoid a black cat crossing my path.

It was Lent, about four weeks before Easter. This was the time of the year when Baba Dochia throws off the first of her winter furs. Baba Dochia is a mythical figure, but we in the village believed in her as firmly as in all the other superstitions and fairy-tale characters. The legend has it that she sits on the highest peak in the Carpathian Mountains, wearing thick layers of furs to protect herself against the intense cold. Every year on her Name Day, which is the first of March, she discards the first of her furs, and she throws off the others one by one every few days until the spring equinox. So if it grew perceptibly warmer in the month of March, Baba Dochia was thought to be kindly disposed and the harvest promised to be a good one that year.

One Sunday I stood at the open window and I
was glad to see that there was noticeably less snow
in the streets than there had been earlier. It seemed
to be getting warmer too, and I knew that Father
and Mother would take it as a good sign that the
weather was improving in accordance with the
legend.

As I turned back into the room, my glance fell
on the clock, just as the minute hand was moving
forward. That was another of our village superstitions and it meant that you were going to see someone very dear to you that day.

It must be Nadine, I thought. I had been invited there for the afternoon. Then I laughed at
myself for being so ridiculous. Why, I saw Nadine
every day! But there was no one else I could think
of. Kuza was not in town and my parents would
be busy in the kitchen painting Easter eggs, as
they always did on the Sundays before Easter.
"Don't be so superstitious," I told myself, but I
did not listen to my own advice. All the way to the
Jeschans' I kept thinking about the clock hand.

I rang the bell at the garden gate. There was a
soft humming as the gate opened and I walked up
the broad path. Nadine came running to meet me,
wearing a frock of pale silk. Her auburn hair
waved around her narrow face, on which all the
features seemed to have been finely penciled in.
There was nothing large or robust about Nadine.
I cannot describe her, but she always gave me the

impression that she had never had to make a strenuous effort in her life, that it would be wrong if she ever had to do any real work. You could not imagine her laboring in the fields or even gardening. I could only think of her dancing, or lying on an elegant couch, reading. Nadine needed a shining frame, like the pictures in the hall, I thought, as she came toward me. Perhaps the stage would provide her with such a frame, or a lovely room, or a flower garden.

"Annuzza!" she called to me. "We have a visitor. It's Cornel, my cousin from Bucharest. He's been sent to the Military Academy here. He's eighteen and I'm sure he'll end up as a General. I'm dying to know if you'll like him. I think he's rather special."

I did not know what to answer. Now my whole afternoon with Nadine would be ruined. He was sure to be as arrogant and conceited as all the cadets at the Academy. They fairly stumbled over their own feet, they stuck their noses so high in the air. You often saw them parading the Strada Flondor, the main street of the town. They were always interested in the girls from our school, though not us juniors, of course. They had eyes only for the ones who had started wearing high heels and had low numbers on their sleeves. At the end of the fourth year, we had to take an exam we called the *Matura*, and it was only if we passed it that we went into the higher classes and were given lower numbers.

I made up my mind that I would not kowtow to Nadine's cousin, even if he was eighteen. I should treat him exactly as if he were Marcel or any of the other boys from the village school, I decided.

All this passed through my head on the way up to Nadine's room, while she rattled on about his appearance and his manners as if he were a hero in a fairy tale. Suddenly she stopped on the stairs and said, "You do look sour, Annuzza. Aren't you pleased?"

"What about?" I asked curtly.

"About Nelo, of course."

Just like Nadine, I thought, always seeing golden mountains when there were only little hills. As we entered her room I was on the defensive.

A young man got up from a chair. He uncoiled himself slowly, almost reluctantly. Well! I admitted, if you're as tall as the cornstalks in the maize field in the autumn, getting out of a chair must be quite a feat. One Nelo equals two Marcels, one on top of the other, I thought to myself, and smiled inwardly at the absurdity of it.

The tall cousin made a bow, but it was rather offhand. Then he introduced himself, "Cornel Mosdor."

I was so impressed by his height that I very nearly curtsied to him after all, but I remembered in time that he was only a cadet.

"This is Annuzza," said Nadine.

"I thought it must be from your description. So

this is the young lady from an estate in the country," said Nelo, and as he smiled the corners of his mouth dimpled slightly.

What a silly simper, I thought. And what is there to grin about, anyway? Did he doubt that I was a girl whose father was a wealthy landowner? Of course I was. I had been one for the last three years. Master Nelo was just like all the other youths from the Military Academy, with ridiculous golden buttons as big as Drago's *taler* on their uniforms. Nelo's eyes were blue, like Nadine's, I noticed. They laughed in his dark, narrow face as if they didn't quite belong to it.

"If you're as sure of everything as you are about me and the family estate, you must be very well informed," I said tartly.

"Your friend is obviously used to rough riding in the country," said Nelo to Nadine, looking at me all the time.

"No," I said. "I looked after the sheep. That's where I learned a lot."

Nadine looked from one to the other of us in surprise. I felt as if I had stepped on to a stage and was playing a part in a play.

"What did you learn from the sheep?" asked Nadine.

"All kinds of things," I answered shortly.

"I think she is trying to pick a quarrel, Nadine," Nelo remarked, keeping his eyes on me still.

Were people so frank in Bucharest where he

came from? I did not care. I walked over to the
glass shelf and started playing with the little
monkey.

"Do you find monkeys so attractive?" Nelo asked
me.

"Until today, I'd never really met one. The
stuffed ones don't count!" I retorted and no one
was more astonished at my words than I. I simply
did not know that I could behave like that. I suddenly thought of the first time a bird sits on a
branch, and notices that it has wings.

That was how our acquaintance started.

As I lay in bed that night in the dark, Nelo's
dark, narrow face dodged in and out of the familiar
figures of my dreams. I tried to chase him away
but he kept coming back. When I fell asleep, he
haunted me still. He suddenly appeared in front
of a long low-built country mansion, riding like
fury across the grass. Or he scampered like a monkey up into the highest branches of a tree in the
well-kept grounds of a park. Next morning I was
angry with myself. What was Nelo doing in my
dreams? He meant nothing to me, nothing at all.
He was far less important than Marcel, and I never
dreamed about Marcel.

Next day, Nadine said to me, "Nelo thought you
were awfully nice." Although my heart beat a
little faster, I tried to look indifferent as I said,
"I thought he was ghastly. He's just like all the
others."

"But you don't know any of the cadets," remarked Nadine.

"I've seen them. That's quite enough for me," I answered sharply.

"Oh, all right, if that's how you feel. . . ." she said, and we talked no more about Nelo.

Every time I went to the Jeschans', I was nervous in case I had to meet Nelo again. I was terrified he might ask me the name of my father's estate or where it was. Nelo did not look like a person who could be put off with evasive replies. Now there was one more person to whom I had lied, one more who would find out one of these fine days that I was a peasant's daughter.

In the summer you would often find fruit farmers from Oltenia standing at street corners, offering their produce for sale. They wear a curved wooden yoke over their shoulders. From it, at arm's length, hang two big platters of carved wood suspended on four cords, one to the right and the other to the left. These hawkers have to make sure that the weight of the fruit is evenly distributed between the two platters; otherwise it would press too hard on one shoulder. I felt a bit like that myself. I had to see that my fantasy did not outweigh the reality of my peasant origin. It was strange, but after meeting Nelo my conscience pricked me more than ever, and I knew that I was really cheating. If people knew the truth, they would probably despise me.

One day, I went to give one of the younger girls some coaching, and I walked back the usual way to the annex along the Strada Flondor. At that hour, the street was crowded with people strolling about, carefree and relaxed — too crowded, I often thought. Cars and taxicabs used a parallel street for the most part, so that if you were in a hurry, you could walk in the road, rather than be jostled along the pavement. You could see the crowds better from the roadway too, and I loved watching people.

Then I noticed a bunch of cadets approaching. They were eyeing some of the girls from our school and they were laughing. All at once a tall figure detached itself from the others and made straight for me.

It was Nelo.

I felt the blood mounting to my cheeks, and I was furious with myself for blushing. Of course, I had to be wearing an old pair of shoes that needed heeling, and probably my stocking seam was crooked too.

"Are you going for a walk, Annuzza?" Nelo asked me straight out, without any of the customary greetings.

"No," I snapped, "I'm picking violets."

"Now if there's one thing I adore, it's picking violets!" said Nelo. "Do let me help you."

I did not know what to say. Nelo walked by my side as if it were expected of him and he scrutinized the pavements intently.

"It seems to be a bad year for violets," he commented. "I can't see any. Let's go round the corner into the park. We might have better luck there."

"No, I can't." I shook my head. "I must go straight back to the annex."

"Well, if you really must," said Nelo, "we could go violet picking tomorrow."

"I'll be too busy tomorrow."

"Oh, the violets will keep. What about the day after?"

Again I refused. I did not want to make an appointment with him. What would Nadine think? In any case, I felt sure that Nelo would not be paying me the slightest attention if he knew that I was a peasant's daughter.

We had arrived at the corner near the annex in silence and then I said good-bye. It was obvious that Nelo was not used to having people say "No" to him, although I thought that it was rather nice of him to play up to my silly violet-picking story. I wondered what he really thought of me. Then I shook my head impatiently. It made no difference what he thought. Or did I mind, after all?

Two days later I went to see Nadine again and there was Nelo sitting in her room. Nadine left us to get some biscuits and Nelo said to me, "Now I see why the violet girl has no time for me."

I do not know if it was accidental or deliberate, but in the following weeks we saw quite a lot of each other. Nelo often came up to me in the Strada Flondor and walked back with me to the annex, or he would appear at Nadine's unexpectedly when I was there too. We got to know each other better and we had long discussions about the poet Goga and the books we were reading, about school and life in general. Sometimes we even talked about ourselves.

What surprised me most was that Nelo was neither proud nor conceited. He joined in all our jokes as if he were still fifteen, but when we talked seriously, we seemed more like his eighteen.

I only came up to his shoulder and when I stood near him, I always stretched a little to make myself look taller. I sometimes imagined that the other girls looked at me enviously when we walked together in the street.

Sometimes Nelo brought one of his friends, and we either made up a foursome when Nadine had an afternoon rehearsal at the theatre or we went for long walks together. All in all, I had never known such a lovely spring as the one that year. Our village seemed hundreds of miles away. There were times when it ceased to exist altogether.

As I lay in bed at night, I wondered if I were really the same Annuzza who used to walk the fields with bare feet and soles as tough as leather, Annuzza in her dark *katrinza,* stooping by the river to cup a handful of clear water, Annuzza in the maize field or up in the mountain pastures, Annuzza buying beads from Moishe. Was it I who had lived that life and done these things? Or was I the young lady whose father owned an estate in the country?

Fantasy and truth merged only when I became Burda, the well-behaved schoolgirl at the Lyceul Orthodox. Each of my two selves knew the other, recognized one another, but there were two of them all the same, a real Annuzza and an imaginary one. Was it a crime if I preferred the Annuzza I had invented?

The day before we broke up for the summer holidays, I met Nelo once more. He was going to Bucharest and from there to Constanta on the Black Sea.

As he told me of his plans, I thought: He will forget me. When he comes back, he will hardly spare me a glance. Then I shall be able to tell him who I really am. It would hurt, but it would be a relief too. More than ever I understood what Drago meant when he said, "The two sides of life, the dark side and the light, lie closer together than people think," or "We often have to swallow the injustice others do to us, but then, we commit it too."

Nelo spoke very little on that last afternoon before the holidays. Perhaps he was already thinking about his visit to Constanta.

In the Town Hall Square, we saw a group of peasants. They looked just like the men from our village with hard, uncommunicative faces. I looked at their hands and I could see the scars of their heavy work in the fields which I knew only too well. You could tell that the city made them feel uneasy.

Nelo must have noticed it too, for he said suddenly, "It's a terrible mistake to lure people like that into the towns with all kinds of promises and castles in the air. The land is going to rack and ruin and these peasants never really settle down in a town. Do you know, Annuzza, I think that they are like flowers that someone has cut and put in a vase. They look quite nice for a short time, but they soon wither."

But is there no way of transplanting them, of helping them to take root in fresh soil, I wanted to ask him, but I was afraid that I would betray how nearly it touched me, how closely I myself was involved in that very problem. If Nelo suspected that I was a peasant girl, he might not even want to walk with me across the square. I shuddered. I wanted to run away from him, anywhere, farther and farther, until I was safe at home. There I could be myself again, without Nadine and without Nelo.

"Don't you think I'm right?" he went on.

"I don't know," I whispered.

"May I write to you from Constanta?"

I shook my head emphatically and did not speak.

"Well, I shall think about you," said Nelo softly, as we reached the annex.

"So shall I," I said, but I don't know if he heard me, for he had already turned and was walking back the way he had come.

I stood for a moment at the door and watched him, and suddenly I knew that the clock finger had not lied that Sunday in Lent. I had met someone who had become very dear to me.

I dashed up the stairs two at a time as if someone were after me and I threw myself on the bed. What would happen now to Annuzza, the landowner's daughter, and Nelo the promising young cadet?

Chapter 17

KUZA'S WEDDING

WE HAD THREE MONTHS' HOLIDAY in the summer, from the beginning of July until the end of September. It was a long time and, in the first few weeks at home, I thought that it would never come to an end.

Of course, I had plenty to do, helping in the house and the fields. Mother usually sent me home about midday to cook the dinner, and on the way I often stole away surreptitiously into the maize field. I would get out my books and writing things, which I left there in a waterproof bag, hidden under the pumpkin leaves. Sometimes I forgot how late it was and only the striking of the church clock reminded me of my duties. Then I had to run hastily in my soft *opanken* into the kitchen and try to make up for lost time.

Bunika used to shake her head over me, but oddly enough she never scolded. Even Father had reconciled himself to the fact that I was now a pupil at the Lyceul Orthodox, but whenever I arrived home, he reminded me curtly, "While you're here, you won't do any reading or writing or studying. You can do all that in the city. In this house, you'll live like the rest of us."

That was why I still had to hide away secretly in the quiet of the maize field.

One day, I had an idea that would not leave me alone. It was to write the story of my life from the day that the buzzard killed Mikuza, and it was intended for Nadine, and perhaps for Nelo too. Then I should not have to explain things face to face. I wanted to set down everything that had happened, the plain unvarnished truth. It would be much easier to hand Nadine my notebooks with the whole thing in black and white than to stand in front of her and confess my deception.

From that time on, the hours I snatched for myself in the maize field took on a special significance. The pencil wrote down everything I had been through, all I had thought about and dreamed. Behind every word lay a silent plea that Nadine would understand and forgive me.

I had made up my mind to have it finished by the end of the holidays, but then the preparations for Kuza's wedding intervened, and I was caught up in the whirl of activity like a thread of gossamer in a summer breeze. There was no time to run away and hide in the maize field, writing.

In the weeks before her wedding, Kuza's eyes shone brighter than ever. She laughed and sang, and when we were alone in the kitchen she even made me dance with her. Her happiness found expression in every movement, every gesture. Mihai was a peasant's son, and as his mother was no longer alive, Kuza would be the sole mistress on her husband's farm.

I spent many hours of the day helping her to finish off the various gifts that a country bride gives on her wedding day. There were shirts to be sewn for Mihai, his father, and his relatives. For the ushers and the bridesmaids there were long embroidered kerchiefs and every stitch in them had to be worked by hand. That was the tradition and we honored it.

It was also the custom to fill a wedding coffer for the bride's dowry. It was hand-carved and brightly painted and it stood in our bedroom by Kuza's old one, ready to be taken to the bridegroom's house on the day of the marriage.

Puiu sat out in the yard all day painting the wooden plates that were part of Kuza's dowry. Whenever he spoiled one, and that was not infrequently, Bunika would grumble: "It must have been a stupid priest who baptized you, Puiu."

That was our way of saying that someone was clumsy.

One evening, about two weeks before the wedding, Kuza and I were sitting bowed over our needlework, and Mother and Father were discussing the heavy cost of the wedding feast, for they had to invite a large number of guests.

I had never yet heard my parents talking together so heatedly. The words fell fast, like the first drops of rain in a thunderstorm splashing on the baked earth. It was no wonder that I listened.

"We just can't do it," said Mother firmly.

"But we have to, that's all," declared Father.

"A small wedding is better than big debts," Mother persisted.

"Ours is the largest farm in the neighborhood, and we have to make the biggest wedding," replied Father.

"And where's the money coming from?" asked Mother.

"Moishe will let us have it," was Father's answer. The more he spoke, the stronger grew the smell of schnapps in the kitchen. It mingled with the acrid smoke from his pipe. "We'll pay it back after the harvest," said Father without much conviction.

"Your chatter means as little as bird song, man." Mother's voice was angry now. "Use your head, can't you? You know as well as I do that the harvest money is earmarked to buy back the woods that have slipped down your gullet."

The shirt I was sewing slipped from my hands. I looked at Kuza. Her head was bent over her work and she seemed not to have heard. I nudged her with my elbow.

"What's that about the woods?" I whispered.

Kuza shrugged her shoulders.

It was Father who bawled at me, "We're the ones who do the talking in this house! Hold your tongue!"

"Annuzza may as well know that the woods on the hillside aren't ours any more. Every time your father bought a bottle of schnapps, it cost us a tree. Now the woods belong to Moishe and all we have are the empty bottles."

"The crops are the important things. Never mind the woods. Moishe will get his money, don't worry," muttered Father. I had never heard him speak so softly before, as if a guilty conscience subdued his usual loud voice.

"The fields will follow suit if you don't leave off drinking, man," said Mother. She never called Father "Burda" these days, as she always used to. That showed how furious she was with him.

So the woods were ours no longer, the trees I had climbed, the bark I loved to stroke. They all belonged to Moishe now. And in exchange, Father had a collection of empty bottles. I remembered the joke I had once thought of when I first went to Nadine's house three years ago, but it was true now.

"We'll invite a lot of sponsors and they shall pay for it all," said Father.

"And for your schnapps too, I suppose!" cried Mother. "And when the wedding's over, you'll drink away the maize field too."

Not the maize field! Please leave the maize field! I wanted to cry it out loud, but it wouldn't have been any use. I pressed my hand to my lips. In a few weeks, I should be back at school and everything would take its course at home. If Mother couldn't do anything to stop it, how could I? I wondered if I could find a way of earning some money.

Suddenly I realized how much it all meant to me, the farm and the fields, every single ear of corn. For years I had walked across fields and paths and I had known "This soil is ours." Now plot after plot was being sold. Even if Moishe didn't get it, one of the other peasants who drank less than Father would snap it up. Nelo had said, "The peasants are being lured into the city and the land is going to rack and ruin. . . ."

Oh, Nelo, I thought. I know I'm not a landowner's daughter, but if Father goes on drinking like this, I'll be nothing but a beggar's child.

Father went out of the kitchen, swaying slightly. Mother watched him and shook her head.

"Never mind, Kuza," she said as she got up, "you shall have a lovely wedding, I'll see to it," and she left the kitchen too.

"You've been away and you knew nothing of what was going on," said Kuza, stitching away industriously.

"No one said anything to me," I replied.

"What was the point?" asked Kuza.

She was right, of course. It was only that I might have realized much earlier how firmly I was rooted in the soil.

From that evening on, I watched the preparations with different eyes. Kuza seemed less concerned. In her thoughts, she was already the mistress of Mihai's farm. But in everything I did, along every path I trod, I kept thinking, how long can we go on?

Once I met Marcel in the street. I hardly recognized him. He had grown and he was much taller than I. He had been away in Sinaia for two years, serving an apprenticeship to a cabinetmaker. He told me that he had nearly finished now and that he was going to open a workshop in the village. His father would give him the money to start with.

Marcel was noticeably more self-confident than before. He no longer blushed when he spoke to me and he spoke fluently, without hesitation, almost like the young men in the city. His face had altered too. It was as clear and serene as the village pond. But I sensed that he was pleased to see me again.

"Your sister has asked me to be one of her ushers."

"Oh, I don't suppose she knows anyone else."

"Maybe she does, but she thought that you would like it. I'm pleased, at any rate."

I nodded, but I did not know if I was pleased or not. This was Marcel, not Nelo. But Nelo had probably forgotten me in fashionable Constanta on the Black Sea. There must be lots of girls there, real landowners' daughters.

At least Marcel knew who I really was. I did not need to act a part in front of him. This was where I had lived my life and I could speak without fear of giving myself away. Yes, I was glad, after all, that Marcel was to be Kuza's usher and that I would be a bridesmaid too.

A few days before the wedding, Marcel and the other usher, a friend of Mihai's, rode round the countryside to invite the guests. They wore their Sunday shirts and embroidered trousers. Kuza and I pinned flowers in their caps and on their jackets. As they set off on horseback from our house, I handed Marcel the traditional little flag the "bidders" carried, a brightly embroidered piece of cloth tied to a short stick. Both of the young men had painted wooden flasks strapped to the harness. They went their rounds on three consecutive days, always starting out at the same time of day. They called at the scattered farms in the neighborhood or they stopped people in the streets and offered them a drink from the wooden bottle. To take a drink was the same as accepting the invitation.

At home, we were busy preparing the house and the courtyard for the festivities. It was the tradition to make these as lavish and as boisterous as possible, for one of our superstitions was that the noisier the wedding, the more tranquil would be the married life of the young couple.

There was much cooking and baking to do and tables to be set up. I kept asking myself where Mother got the money for it all, but she said no more about it, and I did not dare to ask. Bunika sat in her usual place, ordering everybody about. Father had to sample the wine and the schnapps. Twelve of our neighbors had been invited as sponsors, as was the custom, and they would meet the bulk of the expenses.

Kuza got up early on her wedding day and I watched her making herself pretty for the great occasion. She touched up her lips with beetroot juice to make them glow deep red and she pinned fresh poppies and cornflowers into the crowning braids round her head. There was a dazzling nosegay of flowers at her belt too. I got up and dressed in my new *katrinza* and heavily embroidered blouse. This time we both wore silk stockings and low black shoes.

Puiu was harnessing both horses and he stuck flowers in their manes, singing:

There's a wedding today. No work. Hurray!
The dowry is rich. There's a wedding today!

At ten o'clock, Kuza stepped up onto the bridal wagon. Her face was radiant. The cart was so thickly garlanded with flowers and sprigs of fir and ribbons that you could not see the woodwork at all. Behind Kuza stood the wedding coffer filled to overflowing.

The bridegroom's wagon was already waiting in the road by the gate. Kuza led off, standing and waving to Mihai, who followed a short distance behind. All the carts that had been waiting, lined up in the roadway, formed into a grand procession. I was on the third one with the two ushers. After us came my parents and Mihai's father, then the sponsors and the other guests and finally the boys and girls who sang all the way. All the carts were festooned with ribbons and flowers. It was a cheerful sight.

When we reached the church, there was a crowd of spectators. We went inside quietly and Father Stanescu began to say the wedding Mass, which takes two hours. Once, Marcel bent his head down to whisper, "I wonder if we'll be standing there like Mihai and Kuza one day."

"Ah, but with whom?" I replied softly.

"You and I together of course," he retorted, still whispering.

I shook my head so hard that a flower dropped from my hair. Marcel stooped to pick it up. As he gave it back to me he said, "You'll learn, one of these days!"

I did not answer, but I thought that it must be lovely to get married when you're happy.

When Mass was over, the priest exchanged rings as the symbol of the spiritual betrothal and then followed the wedding ceremony proper, the laying on of the marriage crowns. Two wooden rings are used for crowns, which the priest places on the heads of the bridal pair. Then the priest and the choir sang the traditional "Isaiah dances, Isaiah dances before the Lord." This is an ancient ritual, older than Christianity itself, and its origins have been lost. It is both solemn and gay. The priest takes off his stole and passes it to the first sponsor, who hands it on to his neighbor and so on, right round the whole congregation. Then everyone clasps hands and circles the decorated altar three times.

To conclude the ceremony, the priest took down the white wax candles on which a colored pattern had been painted and handed them to Kuza. I saw that her eyes were moist. These candles had been standing on the altar throughout the service, throwing a soft glow on her face. She and Mihai would give them a place of pride in their parlor for the rest of their lives.

We all left the church and drove back to the farm in the order in which we had come. This was the first time I had ever taken part in a wedding, and I thought that I had never witnessed anything more impressive and beautiful.

When we got home, the rooms and the courtyard were full of tables already set. Neighbors had loaned us extra tables and dishes and cutlery. The white tablecloths glittered in the midday sun.

The table in the parlor was reserved for our "distinguished guests," as Father called them. They were the priest, the teacher and Burgomaster with their wives, the doctor, and the chemist. There were more tables in the hall, in the kitchen, and out of doors. The biggest table was in front of the veranda and that was where Mihai and Kuza sat, holding hands as if they could not bear to be parted.

The feasting went on until evening and the musicians did not stop playing. When all the food had been eaten, Father and our two farmhands served the wine. Then he asked Marcel to start collecting. Mother handed him the tray on which was the beautiful cut-glass goblet we called the Pahar Dulce. It was filled in the traditional way with fruit and wine and offered to each of the sponsors.

I had to admire the way Marcel went up to the first sponsor and his wife, without a trace of self-consciousness or embarrassment. He really has changed a great deal, I told myself. In a clear voice he called on the sponsor by name and offered him the glass. We all waited in silence as the man and his wife emptied it and he cried: "Long live the bride and bridegroom."

Then the sponsor placed several bills on the tray and announced that he would also be giving the young couple a calf and three sheep as a wedding present.

Meanwhile, the other guests had come out into the courtyard, the "distinguished visitors" included. Everyone crowded round and clapped and cheered as the sponsors named their gifts, and the musicians played a rousing fanfare.

So it went on. The goblet was refilled each time and one sponsor after another said what he was giving and placed some money near the glass. Then the second usher went the round of the remaining guests, collecting their contributions on a big wooden platter.

I sat in my place and watched Father pocketing the money and Mother nodding approval. Kuza and Mihai were too wrapped up in each other to take much notice of the generosity of the presents.

I wondered what Nelo would think of getting married in this way. It was a typical peasant wedding, like all the others in the neighborhood. All the same, it made me feel rather uncomfortable. It looked like downright begging under the bright cloak of a wedding although, to be honest, I don't suppose I should have given it a thought unless I had heard that conversation of my parents a fortnight before.

"It's a handsome wedding," said Marcel as he came back to the table. I nodded. Would the wedding of a landowner's daughter be anything like this, I wondered.

"Tell me, Annuzza, would you mind marrying a man who wasn't a peasant?" Marcel asked me.

"I'll never marry a peasant, you can be sure of that," I answered.

"Good!" declared Marcel, laughing.

"Nor a carpenter either," I added.

"A cabinetmaker's different," said Marcel and tried to take my hand.

I jumped to my feet quickly and escaped. Mr. Morianu was standing close to the veranda and I ran to greet him.

"I hear you're doing very well at school, Annuzza," he said. "If you go on like this, you ought to get a University scholarship."

What would he say, I wondered, if he knew that I was telling a pack of lies to my best friend?

"I might go as a governess on some country estate," I murmured.

"I expect a good deal of water will flow into the Black Sea before you really know what you want," said Mr. Morianu.

Down to Constanta, I thought.

Then Marcel found me again and persuaded me to dance. Did I only imagine it, or did I really fly light as a bubble over the green grass? I seemed hardly to touch the ground. And with every whirl, my thoughts grew more and more confused. This was Kuza's wedding day. Why shouldn't I enjoy

myself for once, and forget about the woods that
had been sold, about Nelo and Marcel and Nadine?

A crowd of villagers had gathered outside the
fence to watch. The music sang out into the evening and there were even people dancing in the
fields. Then I saw Kuza take Mihai by the hand
and lead him to the gate. They opened it together,
laughing, and they let everyone in to mingle with
the invited guests.

That is the way it was in our village. No one
must be left out. We all belonged together and the
gates must be opened wide.

At midnight, we all stood round in a circle while
Kuza and Mihai danced the bridal dance. The
stars twinkled like distant candles.

As it came to an end, Mihai took a silk hand-
kerchief from his belt and tied it round Kuza's
fair hair. As a married woman, she must not be
seen with her head uncovered. So it was that Kuza
received the symbol of her new status at her
husband's hands and she would wear a kerchief
for the rest of her life. On weekdays, of course, it
would be a plain woolen one, but I knew that
Kuza would treasure the silk scarf as long as she
lived and keep it safely in her wedding chest.

From that moment too, Kuza ceased to be a
member of our family and entered her husband's
instead. Like every peasant's wife, she would have
to manage the farm's affairs. Her life would not
change in essentials; the cares and joys would

remain the same, but hers would be a different household now.

The feast lasted until the early hours of the morning and the sun's disc glowed over the yellow fields. It shed its light over weary figures, lolling on chairs or sitting on the ground. A few people were still dancing, and the musicians still played tirelessly, but the tables were half empty and I noticed that the cloths were stained with brandy and wine.

Father sat hunched up on the veranda steps. His shoulders drooped like the withered flowers in his tall cap. As I went past him into the kitchen, Mother came up to him and said, "You've had enough, man. You'd best be going to bed."

"You can't tell me what to do, you're not the priest," he babbled. "I'm staying here. It was a fine wedding, a beautiful wedding. Annuzza's will be like that. She shall marry Marcel. That's right, Marcel. . . . Her wedding will be bigger still. The Burgomaster has lots of money, enough for the woods and the maize field and for schnapps too . . . plenty of schnapps . . ." Father's tongue kept getting in his way.

I was horrified. It was true that he hardly knew what he was saying, but suppose Mother agreed? She was sober enough. I wanted to hear what she had to say.

I stood there gripping the doorpost tightly. I was not going to be promised and sold so that

Father could get drunk, and certainly not to
Marcel! What would he or his father think if
they had heard Father speaking like that?

Mother said nothing. She took Father by the
arm and tried to get him to his feet.

"Did you hear what I said, woman? I'm going
to find the Burgomaster to tell him that Marcel
shall have Annuzza. Where's he gone?"

"The Burgomaster has gone home and don't
think that I am going to let you sell your daughter
while you're tipsy, the way you sold the woods.
I'd be glad for her to marry Marcel one day — he's
a decent lad. But she needn't do it unless she
wants to, do you hear? You won't interfere, and
neither shall I. And now come on. Get to bed."

Father swayed to his feet. "It was a splendid
wedding . . . a lovely wedding . . ." he muttered.

I ran through the kitchen and into my bedroom.
It was true that I could not fall round Mother's
neck and hug her, but I was deeply grateful to her
nonetheless. Suddenly I was aware that she must
be watching over me. But what if she found out
about the falsehoods I had been telling Nadine all
these years? The city was far away and my foot-
hold there was precarious. This was my home. I
knew it more surely than ever.

As I lay in bed, it occurred to me that my school-
ing might be a means of doing something for
Mother and the farm, but even next morning, I
could not see how.

Chapter 18

THE EASTER
CANDLE

WHEN I WENT BACK TO SCHOOL after the summer
holidays, my life continued exactly as before.
I studied, I went to see Nadine, and I waited
for Nelo to come back from Bucharest.

I spent many afternoons writing my life story for
the two of them. I worked as hard at it as I'd ever
worked at anything in my life — even the entrance
examination three and a half years before. When I
came to the time I had started high school, I could
not help seeing at once how much easier it had
been for me to write about the village and my life
and thoughts as a peasant child. It was obvious
that nothing in the city was important to me per-
sonally except my friendship with Nadine and
Nelo. They were the only people here who meant

anything, whereas at home there were so many familiar figures: my parents, Kuza, Bunika, Puiu, Drago, the teacher, and the priest — even Moishe. At home there were the hens and Huzu, the mountain pastures and the village itself, the river, the feast days, and the maize field, my maize field.

If Nadine turned away from me, I should be quite alone in the city once more.

One day, Nelo came back from Bucharest. I happened to be at Nadine's, and he walked into the room quite unexpectedly. My heart began to throb so loudly that I thought everyone else must hear it beating as distinctly as the ticking of a clock.

"Hello, Annuzza. Have you had any luck with your violet-picking recently?" he asked me softly when we had shaken hands.

I shook my head, but it pleased me to think that he had not forgotten our first meeting in the Strada Flondor. I could remember it too. Whenever I thought of Nelo, I could recall simultaneously all the times we had met and everything we had said to each other.

"Nor me," he said. "In fact I haven't found a single violet all summer," and he gave me such a look that I blushed. It seemed only yesterday that he had said good-bye to me.

We saw each other often at Nadine's that winter, and when we met we always had a lot to talk about. Sometimes Nadine said, "I don't think Nelo would come here nearly so often if it were not for you, Annuzza." I denied it emphatically, but the thought of it was far from displeasing.

I had made up my mind to give Nadine my notebooks just before the Easter holidays. I was not looking forward to it, but at the same time, I wanted to get it over with. As I lay in bed, trying to get to sleep, or when I woke up in the mornings, I kept wondering how Nadine and Nelo would behave toward me when they knew the truth. There were times when I believed that they would understand and there were others when I was equally convinced that they would turn away from me. I veered from one mood to the other like rain and sunshine, like good and bad harvests.

I seldom bumped into Nelo in the street these days. He was working hard for his finals at the Military Academy. But I met him by accident just before Easter and on the very day that I had finished writing my story.

We walked together for a little way without speaking. Then Nelo said, "You seem different today, Annuzza."

"The holidays start in four days' time."

"Don't you like going home, then?"

"No, it isn't that," I answered softly. "It's coming back that I'm worried about."

"Why?" he asked.

I could not explain, so I did not reply. He would soon read it for himself.

Nelo did not press the point. On the contrary, he

seemed eager to change the subject and said, "If I get through my exams, I shall be made a lieutenant in a month or two. Might I come and visit you at home during the summer holidays?"

I had heard those words so many times in my imagination that they had a familiar ring.

"If you still want to, in the summer. . . ." I answered.

"Why ever not? Summer's the best time. I'll be delighted to come then," said Nelo laughing.

"In that case, I'll be very glad, too," I murmured.

But I knew he would never come, not when he had read everything. Or would he? Could he possibly like me for myself and not for my country estate? Perhaps he really did not mind who I was and where I came from. I knew that I would not care, if he were only a simple peasant boy! But there stood between us the endless path of deception.

We said good-bye to each other, for Nelo explained that he would not be able to come to Nadine's before school closed. He had his written exams during the next few days.

"I hope you get through," I said.

"I think I ought to," said Nelo; "and I do hope that when you come back, you won't be so depressed."

"Oh, Nelo!" I said. "So do I!" He could scarcely know how much I wanted it, almost as much as my other wish, that Father would not drink the maize field away.

Before I left for home, I gave Nadine my manuscript. It was as difficult as it had been to give up the beads I had bought with stolen money all those years ago.

"It's the story of my life," I said. "Please read all of it, and when I come back after Easter, I want you to tell me what you thought of it — everything, mind you."

Nadine looked very surprised. She shook her head and started to turn the pages inquisitively.

"Not now," I begged her hurriedly. "Please, not today. Promise me you won't start it until tomorrow."

"You are funny, Annuzza," said Nadine, "but if it means so much to you, I'll promise."

When I left, my notebooks lay on a table in Nadine's room. I can't quite describe it, but I had the feeling that part of me was free at last and could soar into the air, but at the same time, that I was bogged down, up to my knees in mud and I could not free myself.

A dark chapter of my life came to an end as I handed my notebooks over, but I went on writing all the same. I knew by then that it was not only for Nadine and Nelo that I had put it all on paper. It was mostly for myself.

During Holy Week, I went to see Kuza several times. Her home was scoured and polished till it shone and Kuza's face was a picture of happiness. Mihai and his father were out working in the fields and I helped Kuza paint the Easter eggs. We boiled the eggs hard and dyed them. Then we drew patterns and flowers and animals with a quill dipped in hot wax. When they were finished, we arranged them on a wooden dish, just as we had always done at home.

As we sat side by side and the pile of finished eggs grew, Kuza said abruptly, "You ought to come back home, Annuzza."

I was very surprised. "Why?" I asked. I had always thought that Kuza more than anyone was glad that I had the opportunity to go to high school.

"The farm is slowly going to pieces. I don't think that Father sees any sense in keeping it up, now that you're away. That's why he drinks all day. I'm married, you're away at school, and Puiu has always said that he'll never stay in the village. If you were there, Mother would have less aggravation and you could take over the whole farm eventually."

"But I have my scholarship, Kuza," I objected.

"Yes, I know," said Kuza, "but think it over anyway."

I nodded. I had thought about it a lot already, but it had never occurred to me to give up my scholarship and come home. What was more, I did not really think that it would have the slightest effect on Father. If I came back to the village now, everyone would laugh at me, and the years I had spent in the city would be like a barrel with a hole in the bottom. Everything that had been poured into it would trickle out again, and it would soon be as empty as if it had never been filled.

Kuza's words haunted me all through the holidays, and I could no more forget them than stop wondering what Nadine and Nelo were thinking about me by now.

On the Wednesday before Easter, Puiu and I went down to the river. He was carrying a linen bag with eggshells in it. We knelt together on the bank and threw the shells one after the other into the water. The legend had it that there were people living downstream who had neither priest nor calendar and the shells would bring them the tidings that Easter was coming. No one knew for sure where these people lived, nor indeed if they actually existed, but we cast the eggshells into the water, because it was an old custom.

Puiu and I watched the fragments drifting downstream, light as paper boats dancing over the ripples.

"Do you still want to be a shepherd, Puiu?" I asked him.

Puiu nodded. "Either a shepherd, or a vagabond going from place to place until I've seen the whole country."

"But that's not a career," I objected.

"I don't see why not," said Puiu. "It's what I want to do and I shall do it."

Kuza was right, I thought. Puiu would never stay in the village. There would be no one to take over the farm. Perhaps it really was up to me to stop the rot. I decided that I would go to Father Stanescu for advice.

But on Thursday evening, the Easter celebrations began and I had to wait. The whole ritual from the Crucifixion to the Resurrection was one I had known from childhood. The great bell was silenced from Thursday evening until Saturday midnight. On Good Friday, the small bells were tolled to mark the burial and then only for a short time. When they stopped, the sound of two wooden mallets beating against a free-swinging board in the church tower could be heard like rhythmic drumbeats all over the village, calling us to prayer. At church, the priest read the Gospel of the Passion and Death of the Saviour in several languages. I stood near Mother and saw her fold her work-roughened hands as she prayed. Her face was lined with worry. Was it up to me to help her?

As in previous years, we all went to church at midnight on Saturday. My parents were there with Bunika and Puiu, and Kuza and Mihai joined us with his family. As the liturgy was sung, the full peal of the bells that had been silent for three whole days rang out, and from the church went up the cry: *"Christo a inviat — Christ has risen!"*

To which the whole congregation responded: *"Adeverat a inviat — Truly He has risen!"*

Then we took long wax tapers and lit them from the altar candles. The priest left the church followed by the choir, and we filed out behind them. The choirboys sang and the candles flickered under the dark night sky like a rippling pool of light. Three times we had to circle the church, holding our candles in front of us. You could make a wish and if the flame was still alight when you carried it back to the altar, your wish would come true. I believed in this with all my heart, and as I lit my candle at the altar, I had only one wish, that Nadine and Nelo would understand and forgive me.

Puiu and I were among the last in the procession, with a solid stream of people ahead of us. The sight of them moved me as it did every year. The tiny flames spurted in the cool wind. I placed one hand round mine protectively. Never before had I been so afraid that it might go out. The wind blew strongest at each of the four corners of the church and, every time we turned a corner, I held the light as near me as I could and shielded it with my arm. I could see Kuza, who was just in front of me, silently moving her lips and watching her light anxiously. I wondered what she was wishing.

We had been round twice and here and there a light had gone out. You were not allowed to re-light it, of course. The flame of my candle swerved to one side and it reminded me of Nadine dipping and swaying in some complicated ballet steps. Or of Nelo, who was so tall, bending over to tell me something. For a moment I was back in the city and I must have moved my hand away. A gust of wind caught the tiny flame and blew it out.

Tears started to my eyes. I stopped. My darkened candle felt like a dead stick in my hands. Nelo would never forgive me. I had lost him, I knew it.

In the week that followed at home, all I could think was that everything was over, and the picture of the lifeless candle haunted me. My dream had gone out with the flame. Even so, I kept telling myself that it had gone out right at the end, and at a moment when I was not quite concentrating on my wish.

The evening before school started I went to the church again. It was not to consult the priest, but to go through the burning candle ceremony once more, alone this time. I was going to give myself a second chance.

I lit the altar candle with a match and held mine in the flame until it caught. Then I went out into the twilight. It was not quite dark and I hoped that no one would see me. My heart beat fast with excitement. I moved cautiously and the air was still. I thought only of my wish and my dread that the candle would go out again. When I reached the church door for the third time, it was still alight and I was sure that everything would come right after all. I laid my candle gently on the altar.

As I turned to go, a side door opened and Father Stanescu appeared. He saw me at once and asked me what I was doing. I hesitated, and then I blurted out the truth. The priest looked hard at me for a moment. Then he said in a serious voice, "You can't deceive God with a trick like that, Annuzza. If your Easter candle went out, you must face up to it, my dear."

Was he right? I did so want to believe that it was the second candle that counted, not the first. My wishes were stronger than Father Stanescu's warning and when I went back to town next day I had not lost hope.

Chapter 19

BACK AT SCHOOL

GROWN-UP PEOPLE always seem so sure about right and wrong. At least they behave as if they are. I realized which was which too late. Otherwise, it would not have been such an ordeal for me to go back to school.

Despite the promise of the second Easter candle, I was dreading the first meeting with Nadine after the holidays. My footsteps grew slower and slower as I approached the school building, but presently I was standing at the classroom door as I had done so often before, although it felt different today, almost like the day of an important exam.

I wondered if Nadine had come yet. I turned the door handle automatically and, as I went in, I saw the familiar faces. Most of the girls were sitting at their desks or standing about in little groups, talking. Everything seemed slightly blurred to me, as if I were looking through a veil. There was no sign of Nadine. The double desk we shared was empty. I hung my satchel up and sat down with my head in my hands. Perhaps she was chatting at the other end of the classroom, but I had not the courage to look round and find out.

"There you are, Annuzza!" I suddenly heard Nadine's voice behind me.

I turned round and I saw that she was making an effort to look natural as she came toward me, but she could not quite manage it.

"Did you have a nice holiday?" she asked. "How's your sister's new farm? Is it big? And what about Mikuza the Second? Is she laying well?"

This was awful. Was that all Nadine had to say to me? Did she really want an answer to all those silly questions? What ought I to say or do? I felt as helpless and weak as a chicken straight from the egg. Nadine was talking to me, it was true, but there was a gulf between us.

"Nadine," I said, and I hardly recognized my own voice, it was so low and shaky, "are we still friends?"

Nadine looked straight past me and tried to laugh. "What on earth do you think? Of course we are! I know Mummy said . . . but she often says such funny things. I'd love to come and see your farm one day, and you can take me up into the mountains to see Drago. I'm dying to try *mamaliga*, you know. And by the way, my father often has a drink too, liqueurs and things. We've heaps of empty bottles in the cellar, I can show you . . ."

"Are you furious with me, Nadine?"

"No, of course not. Why should I be?" Nadine kept playing with a pencil, fidgeting on the bench. She was chattering away, but she was saying nothing.

"Honestly, I don't mind a bit. I know Nelo thinks that you should have told us ages ago, that it's all right to pretend so far, but there's a limit . . . oh, never mind what Nelo thinks. It doesn't matter a hoot."

"But it does. It's very important." I said simply what I thought, but it might have been better to hold my tongue. I told myself that I did not know what either of them really thought, but in my heart of hearts I knew that it was all over. Nadine would never come and visit me in the village. She would loathe *mamaliga* and the walk up the mountainside would tire her long before she reached Drago's hut.

"Oh, don't let's bother about it now. We can have a good talk some other time, if you insist."

I nodded. What else could I do? I saw that Nadine was trying to skate round the difficulties, but neither she nor I could pretend they weren't there. Mother had once broken an earthenware jug, and as she stuck the pieces together again, Bunika had muttered from her window corner, "It will never hold hot water now. A thing that's mended can never be whole again."

It was the same with our friendship. It was only patched up. Nadine had tried to mend it with words, but they could never make it whole again.

I felt it more than ever in the days that followed. In spite of all the homework I had to do and the tutoring I did, the afternoons were empty. Nadine did invite me around once, but my refusal did not seem to upset her very much. She did not ask me a second time. We still talked to each other at recess, but everything between us had changed.

I had not seen Nelo yet. Every time I walked along the Strada Flondor I looked for him furtively. I longed to see him and to speak to him. I wanted him to face me and say outright that he had misjudged me, that he did not understand me at all.

One afternoon I caught sight of him with a crowd of young men on the opposite side of the street. It was like our first meeting, except that he was now wearing a lieutenant's uniform, so he must have passed his exam. I would have given a great deal to be able to go over to him easily and naturally and congratulate him. I don't think that he saw me at first, but then he happened to look up and he seemed to be staring straight at me. My knees trembled so that I could not move. He raised his cap and bowed and all I could do was to bow back. I saw him excusing himself to his friends and coming toward me. I stood there, rooted to the spot. I felt ashamed of myself. He would be bound to think that I was waiting for him.

"Good afternoon, Annuzza," he said, not looking at me. "I think that I ought to tell you myself."

"What do you mean?" I asked, and was surprised that my voice was so calm.

"That I shall not be able to pay you a visit this summer as I intended. . . ." As he said it, he looked down at his gloves. They were snow white, immaculate. It was odd that at such a decisive moment I could take in such petty details.

"That's what I expected," I said tonelessly.

"Yes, I know you did. That's why I can say it frankly. I'm sure you understand."

I nodded. "Yes, I understand."

"I'm leaving for Ploesti in a few days, my first posting, you know," Nelo went on, trying to make conversation.

"I wish you the best of luck," I said, "in everything."

"Thanks."

"Well, then . . ." I said, and turned to go.

"Good-bye, Annuzza," he said and there was a sad little smile on his face.

I walked along the street and all round me were people, strangers. There was the noise of traffic, of voices, and of laughter. Only I could not laugh.

The hardest thing to bear was the knowledge that it was all my own stupid fault. Everything might have been so different.

My friendship with Nadine and Nelo had started quite out of the blue and it ended as abruptly as it had begun. I might have known it would. Indeed, I probably suspected all those years that it had no firm foundation and would never stand a shock. Perhaps that was why I was so reluctant to speak the truth.

Another person might have squared her shoulders and made a fresh start, found new friends and started to explore the dozens of interests and opportunities which I had simply ignored in my preoccupation with Nadine and Nelo. But I could not begin again. As long as they had been there, the town had worn a smile. Now I had no one and the shadows closed in.

What was I doing in the city?

With my fairy tale of Annuzza, the landowner's daughter, I had myself slammed the door that life had opened for me four years before. Now I stood outside, and like Drago before me, I could never go back again.

Chapter 20

WHERE I BELONG

THE WEEKS BEFORE THE *Matura*, the important examination that took place at the end of the fourth year, were as lonely as my first ones at school. In spite of myself, I hoped for a reconciliation with Nadine, waiting for the day when our former relationship would be restored. Sometimes I thought that I detected a sign of the old friendliness in her look, but then I had to lower my eyes quickly. I was mistaken. On one occasion Nadine passed on to me a good-bye message from Nelo who had finally left the town for his new garrison.

In the weeks before the exam I had to work hard, and any time I could spare was spent in tutoring. The bills and coins in my little leather purse mounted up. I intended to give it all to Mother in the summer holidays so that she could pay off part of our debt to Moishe.

I had not been seriously worried about the exam and I got through quite creditably. Nadine passed too, although she had never been much good at school. On the day school closed, we got our reports and with them a sheet of paper with our new school numbers, the lower ones. Nadine waved hers in the air and danced straight across the classroom with it.

"Mine's a hundred and two!" she announced. "What's yours?"

"Ninety-five," I said.

As for coming to see me during the holidays, Nadine did not mention a word about it. She must have forgotten. It was time for me to leave for home, and I wondered if there was anything else I ought to say to her. All I could think of was, "Have a nice time, Nadine."

"You too, Annuzza," she replied and we shook hands. "You must come and see me again next term."

"Yes, of course," but even as I said it, I knew that I should never go to her house again. As far as I was concerned, the door of her parents' house was locked and I possessed no key to open it. Since Easter Nadine had spoken to me as if through an iron grille. She stood on one side of the railings and I on the other.

That was the last time I ever spoke to Nadine, and my last day at school.

I went along to the market to get a lift home from one of our neighbors who had brought his wagon into town. When I arrived, Mother was in the courtyard, folding up the washing.

"There you are, child," she said as she saw me.

I nodded. I felt all wrong wearing my black school dress and blue beret. I thought that I could see more lines in Mother's face.

"I'll run and change," I said, and went straight to my bedroom.

It was better when I had put on my *katrinza* and peasant blouse. I caught sight of myself in the mirror. With my hair cut short, I was not really a peasant girl. I would let it grow again. I wished it could hide all I had thought and gone through in the city, but that was asking too much. Those memories would remain even when my hair was down to my shoulders.

Gradually I got used to working in the house and the fields all day. One afternoon, as Mother and I were cutting maize stalks in the field, she said to me, "If things go on like this, Moishe will have this field too by the autumn."

I bent low so that Mother would not see my eyes.

"Can't I help?" I asked. "I have some money saved. I earned a bit helping the younger girls with their lessons. . . ."

"That's only a few grains in the sackful," said Mother. "You can't make the liquor cheaper, and you can't quench Father's thirst with words."

What could I say? There must be some way out. I could not bear the thought of selling the maize field. It was the loveliest field in the whole village. Then I remembered that I had intended to speak to the priest at Easter, but I had never done so. Now was the time to do it.

I went to see him that same afternoon. His housekeeper opened the door and showed me into his study. Father Stanescu was sitting at his desk on which stood a silver crucifix. He looked up as I entered and said, "Have you come of your own accord, my child?"

I nodded.

"Then the Lord has sent you."

I stood in front of the desk and kept my eyes on the carpet. It was a big Persian one, as beautiful and as bright as those in Nadine's house. Slowly, as if I were talking to myself, I told the priest my whole story and I did not leave out the part about the lies I had told.

Then I went on to tell him about Father's debts and that we were in danger of losing the maize field, and I wanted to do something to prevent it.

When I had finished, I felt relieved, as if I were no longer carrying my burden alone. Even the stern faces of the saints on the icons seemed to look at me more kindly.

"I need time to think this over, Annuzza," said the priest. "Come back about the same time tomorrow."

"Yes, Father," I answered, and walked away softly in my old *opanken*.

As I turned to go home, I saw Marcel coming to meet me. He waved from the distance and his face shone. You could tell how pleased he was.

"So you're back, Annuzza!" he called out.

"And you?" I asked.

"I've finished my apprenticeship. I'm a cabinet-maker now."

"That's something at least," I breathed softly. "I'm nothing at all."

He smiled at me. "You're Annuzza," he said. "That means an awful lot . . . to me at any rate."

I felt myself blushing. Suddenly I wanted him to read my notebooks, there and then. It could not wait.

"Come back with me a moment, Marcel," I said. I was glad that he did not ask any questions. He waited on the veranda while I got the books.

"I'd like you to read these," I said. "Bring them back to me when you've finished."

He nodded and said nothing. I wondered if he could guess what they contained; but no, that was quite impossible. He tucked the bundle under his arm and said, "See you tomorrow, Annuzza."

I watched him go back to the village by the footpath through the fields. As he reached the bend in the road, he turned and waved to me again. I waved back, but I was full of misgiving. Would I lose Marcel too?

The night that followed was as long and as sleepless as the one before the examination. I knew that a decisive day was dawning.

The church clock was striking four in the afternoon as I faced the priest again. His eyes looked kind-hearted and sympathetic, not unlike Drago's.

"I have been thinking about you, Annuzza, and I have spoken to the teacher and to his wife, and with the Lord too. With Him most of all. The streets in the city are hard, my child. Here in the village, the earth is warm and soft, if you are in sympathy with it. And you are, Annuzza. This is where you belong.

"You have learned a lot at school," he went on, "and I think you are probably advanced enough to help us in a new project here. The government has recently given me the money to open a nursery school in the village. If you care to, I can arrange for you to share the teaching with Mrs. Morianu. Later on, when you are a little older, you would take charge. There are still many unexplored paths here in this village, for you and for us all."

He was silent for a while. I clasped my hands tight. It sounded too good to be true. To stay here in the village with a real job to do, here in my own world! Maybe I could help with the other children too, telling them what it is really like

in the towns, so that they set off fortified with
facts, not weakened by dreams and illusions. In
that way, they at least might find a way of thrusting strong roots into the city's soil, of building
new lives in fresh surroundings. I should be able
to earn money too, and pay off Father's debts. I
could . . . I could . . . No. I mean, I can!

"Would you like to do it?" asked the priest.

"Yes," I replied, softly but firmly, "I would."

Then Father Stanescu asked me to sit down and
we had a long talk. He spoke to me as if I were
already on the staff. I knew that I had a lot to learn
still, but I was glad that it would not be too easy.

When I left the priest's house, the sun was sink-
ing in the west. The village and fields lay before
me as if a magician had painted them bright red.
This was my home, my world. . . .

I went into Moishe's shop. The bell rang shrilly,
but this time it did not make me jump. As he
stepped behind the counter, I realized that the
years had changed him very little.

Before he could ask me what I wanted, I said,
"I have come to tell you that I am going to pay
off my father's debts. I can't do it all at once, but
you'll get your money bit by bit, regularly."

"He owes me a lot of money, you know," he said.
"It's a big sum. . . ."

I pulled out my leather purse and emptied it on
to the counter. "Here is the first installment. Be-

ginning next month, I shall receive a salary from the state. I'm to teach in the priest's new nursery school. And I shall bring you my pay every month. . . ."

"Well, if that the case . . ." he said.

"Yes, that is the case. And my father won't be buying as much of your liquor from now on," I added, as I left the shop.

At supper when we were all sitting around the table I remarked casually, "We'll have to send for my clothes chest from school."

"Why?" asked Mother.

"I'm staying at home. I'm not going back after the holidays."

Father looked up. I saw a gleam of joy shoot up like a tiny flame in his eyes. I had never seen it there before, and it warmed my heart. I saw him get up there and then, and take the schnapps down from the shelf. He opened the window and emptied the bottle into the yard.

A ghost of a smile flickered over Mother's face. Bunika nodded approval and Puiu said, "I only hope the hens don't get drunk!"

Then I told them what the priest had suggested. When I had finished, the room was still. But it was not the stillness before a storm. It was the quiet of the morning before sunrise, the silence of the earth at the start of a new day.

As I lay in bed that evening, it seemed softer and warmer than ever before. Suddenly I remembered that Marcel had not brought my notebooks back. In all the day's excitement, I had forgotten Marcel. Would he come next day?

In the morning I did what I had to do at home and then went to see Mr. Morianu. He gave me a friendly welcome and said, "It's a very good thing all round. You don't have to go and live in the city, just because you've got brains. We can do with you here too, Annuzza."

When I went home again after another long discussion, I could see a fair way ahead. I should concentrate on the little ones, the children of the peasants and artisans, telling them stories, playing games with them, and teaching them their letters and numbers. Two afternoons a week I should take the bigger children and tell them something of what I had seen and learned in the city. The priest and Mr. Morianu both thought that it would be a good idea.

This new life was not the fulfilment of my grandest dreams, but it might be a little dream come true. It was not the big world, but it was my own. I had a job to do, something within my powers.

As I approached the farmyard gate, I saw Marcel standing there and by his side stood the invisible Nadine and Nelo, the town, and the school, and all my lies too.

He did not come to meet me as he had always

done before, but stood there waiting for me to come to him.

"Where are my books?"

"I'm not going to give them back to you," he replied, leaning on the fence.

"Why not?"

"Because you mustn't think about the past any more, only about the present and the future," and his voice was strangely tender and warm.

"Do you think so?" I asked.

"Yes," he replied.

"I'm never going back to the town, Marcel," I told him.

"You'll have to come with me once, you know. We'll have some shopping to do."

"Perhaps," I said. "I may learn in time, as you once said to me."

At least I could make a joke again.

"I must go now. I have some work to do," I said.

"So have I. It's the same for us both, do you see?" said Marcel and he gave me his hand before he went. It was a firm reliable hand. I had never appreciated the strength in it before.

But I did not go straight home as I had intended. I went along the baked earth of the footpath to the maize field. My fingers stroked the tasseled stalks that bordered the path. If I worked hard, the maize field would be mine, and yet ours too, Father's and Mother's and mine.

I sat down in my old place where the juicy pumpkin leaves spread their smoothness, shining like green silk, and I opened one of the small tight corncobs. You could hardly see the seeds yet. Summer was still ahead, the whole long summer and the fullness of life. Every year there would be the harvest feast, the Blessing of the Waters, and the Easter procession around the church. Every year would bring rain and sunshine, sowing and reaping, and the maize field would still be there. I should hear people calling my name: my parents and Kuza, Marcel and the children at school. And if my dreams chose to visit me still, I should bring them here, the old dreams and the news ones too, here into the maize field.

For this is where I belong.